THE SCANDALOUS MISADVENTURES OF HIRAM GRANGE
BOOK 2

HIRAM GRANGE

&

the Twelve Little Hitlers

by

Scott Christian Carr

SHROUD PUBLISHING
MILTON, NH

Scott Christian Carr

HIRAM GRANGE
& the Twelve Little Hitlers

from
Shroud Publishing

You are holding a limited edition small press novella in your hands.
This book is a result of hard work and creative effort.
Enjoy it, and celebrate the possibility of all things.

First Edition

First Printing January 2010
Copyright © 2010 Shroud Publishing
All Rights Reserved

Editor: Tim Deal
Cover & Interior Paintings by Malcolm McClinton
Book Design, Copy-editing & Illustrations by Danny Evarts
Additional Line-editing by Jim Elliott

The text of this book was composed using 12-pt. Adobe Garamond Pro.
Display type was set in Cracked and Charlemagne Std.

ISBN: 978-0-9819894-6-4

Shroud Publishing LLC
121 Mason Road
Milton, NH 03851
www.shroudmagazine.com

ANDY — HAD A BLAST AT CONTEXT!
ENJOY THE BOOK — HITLER WOULD WANT
YOU TO ...!
— Scott Cpr

~DEDICATION~

For my wife Amy, and my children Emmett Zephyr and Eden
Mousley, who offer freely every day all of the things
that Hiram will never know …

For our fearless publisher Tim Deal, who leads the way
with passion, persistence and very much patience …

And for Tusko and Judy, forever trumpeting in the eternal musth …

Also by Scott Christian Carr ...

Novels

Champion Mountain: A Novel of Superhero Family Dysfunction
(Double Dragon Publishing, currently available on Amazon Kindle)

Anthologies

Beneath the Surface (Shroud Publishing)
Demonology: Grammaticus Demonium (Double Dragon Publishing)
Desolate Places (Hadley Rille Books)
Scary! Holiday Tales to Make You Scream (Double Dragon Publishing)
Sick: An Anthology of Illness (Raw Dog Screaming Press)
The Terror at Miskatonic Falls (coming in 2010 from Shroud Publishing)

Comic Books

The Continuing Adventures of Fat Man and Little Boy ...
(appears in *Plastic Farm*, Issue #9 – Plastic Farm Publishing)

Film & Television

Dead Tenants
(TLC television series, Co-creator/Writer)

Junkyard Living
(documentary, Director/Writer)

The Men In the Moon
(feature film, Creator/Director – currently in production)

The Nuke Brothers
(feature film, Creator/Writer, Executive Producer)

The Real Deal
(TV comedy pilot, Co-writer)

*"How little remains of the man I once was, save the memory of him!
But remembering is only a new form of suffering."*

*"I love Wagner, but the music I prefer is that of a cat hung up
by its tail outside a window and trying to stick
to the panes of glass with its claws."*

*"It is the hour to be drunken! To escape being the martyred slaves
of time, to be endlessly and ceaselessly drunk."*

"We are all born marked for evil."

"But a dandy can never be a vulgar man."

—*Charles Baudelaire (1821 – 1867)*

CONTENTS

First little Hitler, tied up in a chair …
Second little Hitler, so full of despair.

Third little Hitler, ever watching the sky …
Fourth little Hitler, only wants to get high.

Fifth little Hitler, all juiced up …
Sixth little Hitler, never signed a prenup.

Seventh little Hitler, walking the dogs …
Eighth little Hitler, the only one who blogs.

Ninth little Hitler, thinks he's Little Orphan Annie …
Tenth little Hitler, lies in snakes with Father Danny.

Eleventh little Hitler, thriving on pollution …
Twelfth little Hitler, invokes The Final Solution.

HIRAM GRANGE

&

the Twelve Little Hitlers

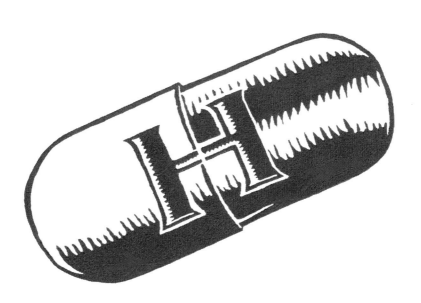

Prologue

In the Abyss, swirling maelstrom and thunderous silence—energy and incense coalesce to form an eye, a finger, a tongue ...

In the Abyss, a minor deity—newborn, yet outside of time—twists and squirms into existence. Opens its single sticky eye, points its single knobby finger and jabbers and waggles its monstrously long tongue. Antimatter smoke and quantum slime take shape, mapped by ancient incantations, predicated by mystical genetic flotsam—and the knobby finger grows longer, the eyeball screams bloodshot, and the tongue runs yellow with fuzzy sores, pustules and plaque—the new-old demon blinks and pokes and issues forth a boisterous Bronx Cheer ...

In the Abyss, predictions foretold and prophesies not yet predicted combine to elongate the ever-reaching digit, run the eye myopic with cloudy pus, dot the wagging tongue with cankerous tumors and boils ... And still the monster stares and prods and drools, its pain growing stronger, its hatred ever more profound ...

In the Abyss, the entity waits and watches, fingers and licks the foul slime from the underbelly of Reality. Decrepit flesh and fungal fingernail merge and slide, growing into an unholy, chitinous member. Not a finger at all, but a throbbing, growing, skin-helmeted battering ram.

In the Abyss, the elongated phallus presses harder against the soft underbelly of the world. Pushing and poking until finally it's through. Dilated pupil peeks through the glory hole into Reality, then pulls back—the beast raises itself, and ... thrusts!

In our world, milky absinthe swirls as iced sugar water drizzles through a sterling silver slotted spoon, louching the hallucinogenic aperitif. A dark figure fastidiously drizzles the water, stirs the liquid ... and then hesitates.

With a heavy breath, young Hiram Grange raises the glass to his lips. Barely old enough to drink, he is nevertheless a seasoned pro. Disheveled, gaunt, and ugly beyond description, his crooked, oversized nose rubs the far rim of the glass. He inhales the absinthe aroma. Tears roll down his cheeks.

He sips, then chugs the green liquid in one long, choking gulp. Winces. He's crying harder now. He drops the glass—it shatters on the floor. Hiram removes a gun from the deep pocket of his overcoat. A huge thing—a black, self-extracting revolver that seems more suited to hunting large game in far-off tropical jungles than riding sidecar in this strange young man's coat.

He puts the barrel to his temple.

'*Interesting,*' thinks the demon, peering from the Abyss, '*Very interesting ...*'

In our world, Hiram closes his eyes. Finger trembling.

He pulls the trigger.

Click.

He drops the gun to the table and fingers the chamber: One empty shell. The shell that took his mother. Hiram slumps to the bar and sobs.

In the Abyss, the demon watches—laughing, pus-filled eye peeping . '*So you're the one, eh?*' it thinks, '*Laughable! You don't look so tough! Stop crying! LOL! Elohelohelohel ...!*' The tongue waggles and lets loose another Bronx Cheer. '*Pbtbtbtbtbbtbt ...!*'

Pressing its single, bulbous eye to the slit in Reality, the demon presses and twists, and peeks into one of many possible futures. *Probable futures.* A future with every likelihood of coming about, should time be allowed to run its course without intervention. *Demonic intervention*, to be precise.

The demon peers into the future: An old man now, Hiram Grange, flowing white hair and beard, stands proud and tall atop one of two shining twin towers. Looking over the city—his city, his country, his world. Hiram the Tall, Hiram the Pure, Hiram the Revered. Hiram the Protector. A powerful nemesis, a force to be reckoned with. A shining figure of holiness and light.

Scepter in hand. Felled demons lie in smoking ruin at his feet. Fallen foes plummet from the precipice of his towers, smashing on the pavement below. Thunderous applause. Confetti and rose petals. A grateful, revering public.

Hiram the Honest, Hiram the Good. Hiram the Holy—a threat to all dark denizens of the Abyss.

The demon shudders, steps back from its peephole into the Potential. Refocuses on the present. Unthinkable that this broken, tainted, pathetic man could ever become what he does. This absinthe-soaked suicidal alcoholic. This perverted sexoholic clown. This cold-hearted, drug-addled sociopathic murderer. *Really?* Not if the demon has any say in the matter …

'*Well then, Mr. Grange, if you and I's gonna be bound up together in 'dis thing, then I think a few changes are in order … I'll take a name in yo speak—one you might get a kick outta …*' The tongue flicks. '*I'll call myself* La Fée Verte. *Apropos, no? The Green Devil …*' The demon laughs, '*Go on! Drink yo drink! Sit up straight! Stop slobbering all over da bar! Man up, Grange … Pbtbtbtbtbtbtbt …!*' The demon sniggers, '*I'll even do ya one better, in our little game. I'll make the first move—show you a glimpse of yo new future, compliments o' yo's truly. A taste of what's in store …*'

'*Wheeeeeee …!*' The demon spins in the swirling Abyss. '*Let the games begin …!*'

In our world, the absinthe takes hold. Grips Hiram's brain in its green vice. Wormwood driven memories float to the surface of his milky brain. The memory: his mother's body lying in a pool of suicide blood and brain matter. The still-smoking gun.

Suddenly, the memory shatters and is replaced by—

—the vision of an older Hiram, more than twice the age of the teenage ne'er-do-well slumped at the bar with the empty drink and empty revolver. The middle-aged Hiram is emerging from a bathroom. Sweaty and out of breath. Even uglier, more wretched, if possible, than he was in youth. Something is clenched in his fist.

Through a hallway strewn with antiques, he strides into a decorated, upscale living room and slumps into a magnificent Mission Oak chair. Stares at his clenched fist and smiles, an expression that looks uncomfortable and out of place on his scarred and misshapen face. With his other hand he pulls a bottle of *Glenfiddich* from the table at his side and brings the neck to his mouth. Then he opens his fist and begins to cry.

In his palm rests a vial. Half-filled with a pearly white, viscous fluid.

Semen.

"Today ..." mumbles Hiram, "Definitely today ..." He takes a long pull from the bottle. Looks at the vial. Takes another inhuman swallow. Chokes. Takes a third. His eyelids flutter. He slumps in the chair. The bottle is nearly empty.

The vial rolls from his palm and shatters on the floor, a sticky mess of glass and sperm. "Then 'gain," he mutters, "S'always t'morrow ..."—

—"The hell was that?" young Hiram raises his head from the bar, back in his own world, his own time. The vision still looms in his head. He pours another glass of absinthe, intent on drowning it.

From the juke, *The Bee Gees* tell it how it is—

> *Well now, I get low and I get high,*
> *And if I can't get either, I really try.*
> *Got the wings of heaven on my shoes.*
> *I'm a dancin' man and I just can't lose.*
> *You know it's all right. It's ok.*
> *I'll live to see another day ...*

With a soft clink Hiram lays the slotted spoon over his new glass. Intricate patterns—overgrown vines and forbidden berries, aloof, mistrustful eyes peering from the dark between the boles of trees—decorate its tarnished silver. Hiram places three sugar cubes on the spoon, and carefully dribbles ice water from a crystal carafe over them. The moment the icy water hits the clear green absinthe a milky eruption occurs. The drink is transformed into a hypnotically swirling nebula. Hiram leans down closer to the table, rapt—white tendrils swim and grope and reach, pushing ever forward to fill the glass. Against his will, the vision returns suddenly, transposed over the mystical drink: his semen spilled in broken glass on the hardwood floor.

Hiram turns and vomits.

In the Abyss, the demon chuckles and moves on. '*Hasta la pasta,*' it thinks, '*Untils we meets again …*' Then, grasping and pulling at the fleshy edges of its poke-hole into Reality, it adjusts its focus and vies for purchase. Pulling the open sore across the underbelly of our world. *La Fée Verte* moves to another vantage point. Same time, different place. Better view. Peeking in, the green fairy (*green DEVIL*, it tells itself) laughs out loud. Bronx Cheer. Drool.

'*Perfect,*' it thinks.

In our world, the demon spies two abominable buildings, jutting into the sky like some stoned, dirty Hippie waving "Peace." Hiram's future throne.

The atrocities dominate the skyline, towering over the vast cityscape. '*This be a powerful spot,*' thinks the green devil, pressing its blood-run eye to the peephole, '*This is a Confluence!*' The demon's blasted pupil widens. '*Or, 'least, 'twill be soon enough …*'

'*All too easy, settin' the dominos in motion,*' the green bastard smirks. Just a little shove to the cerebellum of the soft monkey brain of an angry young revolutionary on the other side of the rock … a subtle tickling nudge, a feathering of the medulla here, a pinching of the pineal there … a crazy notion whispered in the mind's dream-ear in the cold dead of a dark Arabian night ... and, easy as that, bad ideas are set in motion—and decades later, the butterfly wings' flutter in the brain of a volatile madman culminates in a political-societal maelstrom on the other side of the globe.

Planes crash and towers fall.

'*The world will never be the same,*' the green devil grins, '*And I ain't even started yet ...!*' Through the peephole, the beast gleefully watches the chaos to come, in the not-so-distant future. The fruits of its labor, the weaves of its loom. Smoke fills the skyline. '*I'm an artist!*' the demon cackles, spinning in the Abyss, '*I ♥ New York! Wheeeeee!!*'

Bronx Cheer.

When finally the monster regroups enough to stifle all but the most hysterical of chuckles, it floats back to the mouse hole it'd poked. Peers through, an evil eye staring out of a cuckoo clock, looking ahead to the future it is now creating.

On September the eleventh of 2001, the same day that the idea of having a son first fermented in Hiram's drunken brain ('*Oh, where do such ideas come from?*' the demon giggles), the towers are falling, people are screaming, and a dozen young boys are clawing their way out of the Ground Zero debris. Emerging from the rubble. Each covered in dust and trailing tattered jumpsuits. They are identical: darkly oiled hair, in their pre-teens, not yet old enough to shave—and yet ... Could that be ash? Each wears a small, squarish dark splotch on his upper lip ...

As the rescue workers rush in, the children rush out. Scattering in all directions. Losing themselves in the anonymity of the terrorized city.

Twelve identically mustachioed teens.

But that is the future, and this was now.

The green devil shifts the porthole ever so slightly. Same place, different time. Deep beneath Tower Two, still years away from its catastrophic fall, a secret laboratory hidden deep in the bowels of the city. Men and women in lab coats work around the clock. Buzzing like bees in a hive. Worrying over twelve glass canisters.

It is these canisters that draw the demon's eye. Each is filled with a translucent, glowing liquid. Wires and tubes run in and out of them. Bubbles rise and electrodes fire. The green devil peers closer. And staring back, across the bridge of time and reality, are twelve embryos. Pink, bald, tiny … mustachioed .

Cloned from The Man himself. A bad dude whose bad ideas make even the green demon's seem like peanuts, by comparison.

The monster whistles. '*This is gonna be good … oh yes, oh yes … but which one? Which ONE?*'

Shrinking pupil carefully regards each. Scanning for any sign of power or defect. Evil bent or character flaw. But they are identical.

The beast shrugs.

'*Eeney, meeney, miney, moe, catch a Nazi by the toe …*'

And the choice is made. Second Hitler from the left. The demon hones in on its prey. The eye pulls back from the hole, replaced by the green devil's enormous, throbbing member. The beast raises itself, leans forward and … thrusts!

The mustachioed embryo's eyes grow wide. Fetal mouth opens in a silent scream. Tears lost in the glowing saline. A lone bubble escapes the infant's throat as the demon takes the baby Hitler from behind …!

Wheeeeee!!!

...Eighteen Years Later...

First little Hitler, tied up in a chair . . .

J odie. Always, there is Jodie …

Hiram types furiously, fingers dancing over the grime-encrusted keys of his ancient laptop. Burnt-out pixels, sticky trackball mouse. Dial-up—his connection to the larger world is slow, but intoxicating.

You're tied up, he types. *I'm tickling you with a feather. Starting with your toes. Moving up … up … UP!!!*

LOL! replies **jfoster222**. In another window, **FBI-Clarice** writes, *I'm licking my lips, licking your hard, hairy chest … your rock-solid abs …*

My 6-pack, types Hiram. (Never mind his bony rib cage—the gaunt, doughy gut nestled beneath his loosened tie and unbuttoned buttons, sweat-stained shirt, tweed jacket. Shirttails dangling over corduroy trousers. Fly unzipped.) He pushes his spectacles further up the bridge of his sweaty, uneven nose. The anticipation is rising. In another window **jodirocks** writes, *I want you so bad!*

From the radio blares a techno-remix of the *Violent Femmes'* perennial classic:

> *Why can't I get just one kiss …?*
> *Why can't I get just one kiss …?*

Hiram spares a glance at the Mission Oak chair in the corner of the dusty, tobacco-and-opium-infused study. Blue wisps of Presbyterian pipe-weed drift lazily to the ceiling. The opium-infused tobacco burns his lungs, gives his vision a fuzzy, fiery frame.

He regards the antique chair coolly, licking his swollen, oversized fish-lips. In it now, a schoolgirl. Plaid and pretty. Bound and gagged. Tied securely—she bats her long lashes provocatively at him and screams *Do me! Do me! Do me!* with her eyes.

Believe me, some things I wouldn't miss …

Hiram blinks. A wave of weirdness washes over him and he swigs another gulp of *Glenfiddich* to straighten his brain. Straight from the bottle, washing the acrid bite of leftover pills from under his tongue and down his throat. Replacing bitterness with fire.

He's headed for a dark place—the roller coaster is nearing the top of its run, and it's soon to be a long, hard fall for Hiram Grange … a long fall and loop-de-loop. But he'll pull out just before hitting rock bottom. He always does …

But for now, *The Binge.*

I look at your pants and … I NEED a Kiss!

He shakes another pill onto his palm and wags his tongue at the Mission Oak chair—now seating not a schoolgirl but a cheerleader. Not tied, but slouched. Legs splayed in a suggestive rendition of Sharon Stone's *Basic Instinct* striptease.

Hiram swallows the pill and turns his attention back to the computer. His focus is starting to waver. Reality is starting to splinter. Message windows blur, double—keyboard keys dance and trade places. *I'm fliping you over*, Hiram types, never missing the missing "P"—*I'm pushing your face down into the pillow.* And then, in a moment of stoned inspiration, he types, *Are your lambs screaming yet???*

A crash from the bathroom. Breaking glass and a muffled yell. Muted behind the deadlocked door. Hiram pays it no mind. He's on a roll, he's in the zone. He's beyond the point of turning back …

Another message window. This one from **Gashleycrumb**. The message is entirely written in Cyrillic.

Хаве соу фоунд тхем sем?

Hiram tells **jfoster222** that he's naked now. That he's harder than he's ever been.

In the Mission Oak now, a naughty nurse.

Gashleycrumb persists: *Хас хе талкед?*

He warns **jodirocks** to get ready, that he might, just might, be too large for her …

Gashleycrumb replies immediately and in English. *Hiram? Too big? Is that code? What happened to Cyrillic?*

Hiram's hit the wall. Cyber-coitus interruptus. Faux pas. Bad move. Major fuck-up.

Sorry, Mrs. Bothwell, his long fingers dance over the keys. *Wrong window.*

The Mission Oak, empty now. Naked embarrassment temporarily clears his mind of fevered hallucination.

More muffled grunts from the bathroom.

Gashleycrumb responds with a series of question marks, capped with an exclamation point.

Rubbing his eyes, Hiram pulls a small chalkboard closer to him on the desk. Tries to focus. Begins scribbling furiously. The Cyrillic was his idea. He scribbles feverishly, decoding **Gashleycrumb**'s message:

Хаве soy фоунд тхем sem? Have you found any of the others yet?

Not yet, he types. Better to keep it short.

He pops another pill. Takes another drink. *Take off the edge, focus …*

Cyrillic chicken-scratch fills the chalkboard. He continues to translate.

Хас хе талкед?

Has he talked?

Hiram rubs his bony chin and considers his reply. For a long moment he regards the deadlocked bathroom door. The grunting has stopped, but he can still hear muffled movement from inside.

Working on it, he types. Hits REPLY. Slams the laptop shut.

And then, like a cat, he's out of his seat and at the bathroom door—silently and in the blink of an eye. He has a hammer in his hand.

In a blur of motion he throws open the lock, kicks ajar the door and reaches in. Betraying a strength that one would think impossible in such a scrawny frame, he fishes out a man by the scruff of his shirt. Whirls him around and pushes, half-throws, him into the room. The young man staggers backwards. Falls heavily into the empty Mission Oak chair.

Hiram pounces. Raises the hammer menacingly. The boy (in the harsh lamplight of the study his terrified face betrays little more than peach-fuzz, in stark contrast to the dark paintbrush mustache on his trembling upper lip) begins to speak. Hiram raises a finger to his own lips, shushing him.

"Not a word, chum" hisses Grange. "I don't want you to talk. I want you to *think* about talking. Think about what you're *going to say*. Think about telling me where your brothers are. And don't even think about giving me a snow-job, my good man. Even without the mustache, I know who you are. Whose cloth you're cut from, as it were." Hiram raises the hammer as if to strike. "I'll be right back. We're not gonna move now, are we?" The boy shakes his head.

"Good," says Hiram, stepping into the small library (a cramped room that, until recently, served the current, vacationing owners of the apartment as a food pantry). From the shelf he pulls *The Collected Works of Lewis Carroll*. It's a thick book, musty with antiquity, and perfectly sized for a hiding place, a secret compartment of cut-out pages. From inside its covers Hiram removes a plastic ziplocked baggie. Pours a handful of red-capped *Amanita muscaria*—psychedelic faerie mushrooms, and of a particularly potent strain.

He places the book back on its shelf. Then, after a moment's consideration, he removes a copy of *Mein Kampf*. Tucks it under his arm. He might need to refer to it—at the very least, it was heavy enough that he might be able to bludgeon the clone in the Mission Oak chair with it, without doing any permanent damage before he could answer all of the questions that needed answering.

Hiram takes a deep breath. Steadies his nerves. Swallows a handful of the scarlet mushrooms.

After all, no one should have to confront Hitler straight.

Hitler is crying. Blubbering like a baby. Weeping. Tears streaming from innocent eyes. Mustache wet with snot. Jowls jiggling with each sob—bawling. He looks more like an overgrown toddler, a spoiled brat, a trust fund ne'er-do-well—than the teenage monster that he is.

"Shut up," Hiram snarls. "Stop crying. Fer Chrissakes, how old are you?"

"N-N-Nineteen …" the boy stammers. "I'll be twenty in—"

"Shut up, I said!"

"I didn't do nothin', man," Hitler's voice cracks. "Please …"

"The bloody hell you didn't," Hiram levels the book at him. Makes as if to strike. Then tosses it into his lap. The splayed pages of *Mein Kampf* are blurred by Hitler's tears and dripping snot. All but unreadable.

The single-malt psychedelia starts to kick in strong. It's a dangerous dementia. A bad mix. A sweaty, fevered, cold-blooded mean kinda trip. Uncontrollable. Hiram begins to shake. Can't stop sweating. Tries to speak but can't. Tries to ride the wave, but can't—his head goes under. Fists clenching and unclenching at his sides.

His hammer drops to the floor.

Hitler tries to get up, tries to escape. With a detached derring-do, faster than fast, Hiram pulls his piece. His father's gun: Hitler's mouth.

.455 caliber *Webley*.

Five shots. And one empty shell—his mother's shell.

Squeeze—don't pull—squeeeezzzzze … and …

Click.

Hitler slumps back into his chair. Shaking, trembling, sobbing.

His mother's empty shell. Hiram is laughing.

'*I made Hitler cry,*' Hiram thinks. '*I'm making Hitler cry!*'

Hiram is shaking harder now. Sweat pours down his face, stings his eyes. Drips from his chin. He's paler even than usual. He reaches up and wipes his brow and flips the switch on the cord of the recently installed *Mole-Richardson Baby-Senior Solorspot*. A theatre lamp he'd rescued from the dumpster in the alley behind *The Regalia Improv* next door. Illegal for indoor home use. 5,000 watts.

At three feet it can blind anyone insane enough to open their eyes. At three feet, in just 10 minutes, it will cook the skin off of a chicken.

Hiram flips the switch. Hitler is bathed in unrelenting light, an unwilling angel with an unholy halo. Hiram retreats to the shadows, where it's cooler. Diffuser clips and anodized aluminum bounce the light away from him and onto Hitler.

"In 1938," Hiram declares, "Hitler was voted *Time Magazine*'s Man of the Year." No response from the impenetrable hot glow enveloping the Mission Oak. "True fact. Before World War Two the New York phone book had twenty-two Hitlers. After World War Two, it had none." Still no response. "True fact."

"*Can you hear me!*" Hiram screams. The waves of euphoric insanity are coming faster now, harder. "*Are you alive?*" he demands.

"Turn it off!" Hitler screams. Already, the temperature in the room has climbed ten degrees. "It's burning!"

Instead, Hiram reaches over and drops the needle of the *Stack-O-Matic*, filling the room with the amplified earsplitting melodies of Bach's *Toccata and Fugue*, to accompany the blinding glare of the lamp. Much louder here than on his antique Victrola back home …

… for a moment Hiram is swept away in an undercurrent of psychotropic nostalgia—fond thoughts of his old *Airstream* RV. Alone and abandoned. Off-limits. Unsafe.

Being watched.

With a sharp crackle of brain-lightning—the smell of ozone in his nostrils and the musky taste of spores on his tongue—Hiram's fanciful nostalgia is, just like that, ripped away by an undertow of paranoid fury. *How* dare *they drive him away from his home—whoever they are! How dare they force him to break into and squat (unbeknownst to its owners) in this fabulous and fully-furnished upscale apartment? Hiding like a mouse. Like a rat. Like a criminal …*

He'll find them, those watchers, and he'll kill them. Kill 'em all. Murder every last one of the bastards. Whoever they are. Just as soon as he's completed the mission.

The mission? Hiram's drug-fueled revenge fantasy is overshadowed by more pressing issues.

The mission … The mission … His mind is racing, clouded and flowing like melting Jell-O, molten lava. *Mission?* Just what *is* the mission, exactly?

Hitler is screaming now. Begging for mercy.

The squeaky sing-song warble of Gordon Gano and the *Violent Femmes* tries to compete, but is all but lost in the myriad textures of Bach and the terrified and painful death throes of Little H. It's hot as hell in the apartment and Hiram can smell the thick, oily stench of smoldering hair gel. His stomach growls.

Rumbles of desperate, unacknowledged hunger.

He hasn't eaten in days. Can't keep anything down. The hunger is there—but it's overshadowed by the nausea of the mind-candy. The mushrooms. The opium. The tobacco, alcohol and wine. The pills.

There's a subtle, atavistic craving for curry, for the nuclear fury of the Naga Jolokia pepper. For the exotic spices of the Orient—for razor clams, for savory chilled abalone, for takoyaki octopus balls … But then, drowning it all, there is The Binge.

The Binge.

Starving, Hiram knows that he couldn't keep food in his stomach.

Not if his life depended on it. The mushrooms wouldn't let him. The opium wouldn't let him. The pills and *Glenfiddich* wouldn't let him.

The smell of smoldering Hitler wouldn't let him.

There'll be plenty of time to gorge later, he tells himself. Plenty of time for fine dining. For compulsive cuisine. Fast-food take-out and gourmet indulgences ... but for now there is only The Binge ...

The Binge ... and *The Mission.*

Mission? Again, with the mission ... What is the mission?

The mission ...

The mission is sitting in the Mission Oak chair ...

Hitler's *middle name was Elizabeth.*

The *real* Hitler, that is—no, strike that, the *first* Hitler.

True fact.

Hitler had only one testicle.

True fact.

Hitler invented the blow-up sex doll. He wanted to keep his soldiers satisfied and not planting their seed in foreign women. Blonde hair, shaved from imprisoned Jews and bleached. Blue marble eyes. Large rubber breasts, white plastic skin ...

Another pang of hunger. Another wave of nausea. Another true fact. Another blast of crazy.

He'd fed Little Hitler the leftovers of three-week-old kimchee just that morning—coagulated remains in a white Korean food carton.

It had reeked. Still did, but the spices are intoxicating.

He can smell them now.

Burning, uneaten kimchee. Soaked into Hitler's shirt. Cooked under the *Solorspot* theatre lamp. Hiram's stomach growls again.

Hitler had turned up his mustachioed nose to the stuff. "What is it?" He'd eyed the food suspiciously. "It smells rotten," he'd frowned.

"Just eat it," barked Hiram. "It *is* rotten. It's fermented cabbage. You should like it …

"It's like sauerkraut," Hiram had offered.

"It smells awful."

"Then hold your fucking nose."

Hitler had refused.

In a rage of alcoholic fury, at gunpoint, Hiram had forced the rotten cabbage into Hitler's mouth. Smeared it onto his shirt. Mussed it into his hair.

He'd stuffed the foul spiced cabbage between Hitler's molars and cheeks. The young Nazi had struggled to speak. Cryptic, choking words—a warning? A message? A threat?

"*Words* gagh *build bridges* koff *into unexplored regions* blegh …" Hitler had choked, "*Let us never* gulp *forget the duty* retch *which we have taken upon us …*"

A nother wave of mushroom dementia washes over him. The shrooms and the opium aren't getting along. Aren't playing nice. They're playing naughty, crazy games together. And the alcohol is egging them on.

Hiram feels the room stretching out in all directions around him. The wooden floorboards bowing and rippling and sliding in strange tidal waves. His eyeballs are trying to roll out of his head. He clenches his eyelids shut, intent on keeping them in—then worries that they might roll too deep inside—might get lost in the gray tangle of his brains. Hiram can't imagine a worse eternity than being trapped and staring at the dark inner workings of his mind, an unblinking voyeur lost in the maze of his own demons …

It's the asceticism of The Binge. No food. It's the hunger talking—the dirty, unwashed smelliness of his sweat-soaked, unchanged clothes. No sleep, no eat … the wide-eyed horror … The strange, tidal *necessity* of it all … to take it—and keep on taking it—that much further …

The opium and mushrooms are taking over now. Growing roots deep into his under-mind. Hiram can feel the *Glenfiddich* saturating his veins. Seeping into his brainstem, the cradle of life. Feeding those groping, growing roots of psychedelic dementia … Taking hold … He is losing himself. Losing control. Losing his mind, and …

And …

There's only one thing to do. Only one thing to be done. Only one solution …

Absinthe.

The answer would be found at the bottom of a bottle of absinthe. The Girls would know what to do. The girls …

Mother, *Sadie*, and the *Green Fairy*. The Girls …

Twelve Little Hitlers … One down and eleven to go …

Oh, and Jodie … always, there is Jodie …

S taggering down the street, the apartment building engulfed in flames behind him, Hiram spares a glance at a take-out Halal hole-in-the-wall. The smells of marinating meat, shawarma and Jasmine spiced rice grip him to the very core. His stomach rumbles, demanding something more than hallucinogens and alcohol.

Hitler's screams, long since silenced. Only the charred, unidentifiable husk of the clone remains. Melted into the Mission Oak, burned into the floor of the upscale apartment that Hiram had commandeered and squatted inside these past few weeks. Laying low. Now a fiery wreck. Inside, a human cinder, a German charcoal briquette, a burnt, mustachioed marshmallow—just one lone clue to an unfathomable mystery, a leftover booby prize to which the apartment's unsuspecting owners will inevitably return. Burned alive, tied to the ruined Mission Oak chair.

Next thing he knows, Hiram's ducking down an alley holding a Styrofoam tray of Haleem beef, spicy Ramadan Kofta, and Jasmine rice. Fire engines roar past on the avenue as Hiram shovels the food into his mouth. Eating with his fingers. Tandoori and yogurt sauce drip down his chin and stain his suit. His *father's* suit—too snug at his shoulders, but loose at the waistline, held tight by a short length of belt. The cuffs ride high above his ankles and wrists—Hiram's father was a smaller man.

The food is delicious. But the moment it hits his gut, the drugs rebel. As rescue vehicles and police cruisers scream by, Hiram is retching in the alley. Puke stringed with blood and bile. Undigested mushrooms. He presses his sleeve to his mouth, and stops mid-wipe— the hairs on the back of his neck are beginning to tingle. Someone is watching him, he's sure of it. They've been watching for some time now. Ever since all the unpleasantness with Jodie … ever since he'd been forced to abandon his *Airstream* trailer, to flee his home …

Hiram's fingers caress the eight-point-three inch *Pritchard* bayonet in the sheath at the small of his back. Another wave of psychedelia washes over him. The walls of the alley begin to move. The bricks grind against each other, rippling in a lover's caress. The floor of the alley is breathing. The walls are closing in.

Hiram runs for dear life.

'*Too much!*' his mind screams, '*Not enough!*'

He knows what he needs. The girls will have the answer. Jodie (*no, not Jodie, not now—that's what got him into this mess*) … Sadie! Sadie will be able to help him clear his mind. Sadie will put things into perspective.

Sadie will ground him.

Sadie.

And he has something for Sadie. Something special. Something important … (Something in the dark recesses of his mind laughs out loud, a cruel, subconscious *LOL!*)

Sadie.

But first the absinthe …

The woods are dark. Silver moonlight streams between the boles of the trees. A cool, heavy mist runs in lazy, ankle-deep waves over the ground. Insects sing and chirp, throwing desperate, horny mating calls out into the empty night. Perched on a dead-white birch branch, an owl turns its head impossibly around, ever searching for prey.

Hiram is trained to walk silently. To creep. To stalk. It's second nature, even flying as high as he is. He doesn't disturb a soul.

A hundred yards off, in a clearing—a glint of chrome. The silhouette of his vintage *Airstream* trailer.

A tickle in his brain. He knows they're still watching him. He doesn't know who, or where, or why ... (he has his *ideas*: of course, there's the fallout of the *Jodie Incident*, the reason he fled the trailer in the first place. But there's something more at work here. He can feel it ...)

He knows he's being watched. But not by whom.

Or is that just *The Binge* speaking? The mushrooms and opium pulling paranoid strings in his mind? Alcohol pumping strange uneasiness into the pit of his stomach ...?

He can feel eyes all around him.

Pupils dilated, Hiram's intense blue eyes scan the scene as he stealthily approaches the trailer he calls home. The home he was forced to flee. For Jodie ...

All for the love of Jodie ...

Gun in hand—a massive *Webley Mk VI*, the venerated sidearm of the British Army during World War I, chambered with five specially modified .455 caliber cartridges, each hand-scored to maximize their mushrooming effect upon impact. Five cartridges ... and one empty shell. Mother's suicide shell ...

Hiram raises his unarmed hand to the handle of his door.

He grips the handle. The door is ajar.

He opens it a crack. Well-oiled hinges don't make a sound.

Someone is sitting in his study/living area. Watching his TV. Eating his potato chips (kettle-fried, spiced with the rare Grains of Paradise African peppercorns and pure fennel pollen. Very expensive, and very hard to find.)

Hiram steps silently closer. He can hear muffled sobs between the crunching of his exotic, artisan, micro-brewed chips.

Both hands firmly grip his gun.

With the speed and stealth of a trained soldier (after all, aren't all agents of the OIRA trained soldiers? Even the elusive, pencil-pushing Mrs. Bothwell—screen name: *Gashleycrumb*? Wasn't the mission of the misleadingly named *Office of Independent Research and Analysis* to stand guard over the world? Protect it from threats too grotesque for governments to imagine? To police the rips—the *Confluences*—between this world and the realms above and beneath? Realms too unfathomable, too unthinkable for most to comprehend, let alone believe in?) Hiram raises a booted foot and—*WHAM!*—heel meets squarely with the back of the stranger's head.

The intruder tumbles to the floor. Whimpering and cowering. Clutching himself in sweaty fear. Wide eyes pleading for mercy. Snot oozing into his distinctive mustache.

The *toothbrush mustache*. Often referred to as the *Hitler 'stache*, the *Charlie Chaplin mustache* or, for the technical, unimaginative or cosmetically minded: the *1/3 mustache*. The iconic hair sculpture is completely shaved except for three centimeters on the upper lip. The sides are vertical rather than tapered. It is neatly combed and waxed.

That damned mustache.

Competing questions battle in Hiram's mind. Fighting for position on the limited acreage of his tongue. His fingers, clenched tightly on the trigger of the *Webley*, argue for a quick end to all questions.

"What are you doing here?" Hiram shouts. And, "What's the deal with the fucking mustache?" His head is spinning.

The young Hitler is beginning to cry.

"I said, how'd you get in here? Answer me now, dear sir, or so help me, my Paradise chips will make a more than fitting last meal."

Tears and boogers mix with mustache wax and potato chip crumbs. "Are you going to kill me?"

"Yes." Hiram's mind is reeling, his brain feels as if it's simultaneously sweating and rubbing up against a pumice stone. The mustache attempts to scurry across the young man's face and down onto his chin. Hiram clenches his eyes shut. Tries to will the hallucination away. When he opens his eyes, the mustache is back in place.

"Don't move, or so help me you're a dead man," Hiram waves the gun menacingly. The boy nods weakly.

Hiram slides his hand gingerly under the pillow of his pull-down bunk. Comes back with a pair of steel handcuffs. Decorated with pink fur and Dago balls.

"Stand up and hold out your hands."

This is the first time the cuffs have bound a man. First time they've bound a clone. First time they've bound Hitler. '*First time for everything*,' thinks Hiram, shoving the cuffed boy face down onto the couch.

"I just—"

"Shut up," barks Hiram. The walls of the *Airstream* are beginning to ripple and swell. "Did you hear me? Just shut up! How did you get in here? Did I ask you that already? What's your name?" Time is beginning to collapse in on itself in Hiram's sweaty brain. Moments are trading places, square dancing and refusing to make sense.

"Don't move."

"Please don't do this. I'll tell you where the others are. Where my brothers are. I'm the only one who—"

"I said, shut up." There would be time for that after. Time to interrogate the boy. Find the others. Finish the mission. Make Mrs. Bothwell happy. But first, the absinthe.

That's what he'd come for, why he'd risked returning to the *Airstream*.

The Absinthe.

Slumping into his chair, Hiram removes a green bottle from his desk and begins the *Absinthe Ritual*.

Pours the absinthe into a glass. The label on the green bottle reads *Cave de Fayence*. Hiram places his slotted silver spoon on the rim.

Hitler just watches. Hiram has all but forgotten him, lost in the labyrinth of his own mind. His mother's suicide replays itself over and over. The gunshot, the blood, the brains. The cold body slumped on the bathroom floor. The empty shell casing in his *Webley—the suicide shell*. His mother had killed herself—was killing herself. Over and over as time continued its psychedelic loop-de-looping—over and over and over—with his father's gun. And Hiram had never been able, would never be able, to understand why. Or to remove her empty shell.

Her suicide shell.

Sugar cubes and ice. Hiram loses himself in the cold crystal perfection of the cubes for a fleeting eternity. Time stretches out to the horizon of his mind and then rushes past like an eighteen-wheeler on the freeway. Hiram seizes the brief moment of clarity to return to the task at hand: Absinthe.

Hitler is talking now. Jabbering. None of it is making any sort of sense.

"*The green man told me to come here. To come see you ...*"

Sugar cubes in the spoon.

"*At least I think he was green ... at least I think he was a man ...*"
Hitler's words are a million miles and countless dimensions away.

Ice water slowly drips over the sugar. Saturates the melting cubes. Hiram's mind is splintering. Reflections of himself stare back from the murky pool of his mind. He's losing himself. He's peaking.

"*He only spoke through a hole in the wall ...*"

The water drips through the sugar and into the absinthe. The louching process begins. As the essential oils precipitate out of the alcoholic brew, milky white tendrils reach across, filling the liquid green universe. Hiram is transfixed. 'These are my girls,' he thinks. 'My fine and lovely ladies. My green fairy ... Mother, oh Mother ... Sadie, sweet Sadie ...'

"*His tongue ... He told me you could help ...*"

'And Jodie … Always, there is Jodie … I am she and she is me and we are meant to be … Jodie, my love, my desire …' Something stirs in the remnants of Hiram's shattered, dying ego. Something important.

"I wish I could just be happy, like my brothers … find my place …" Jodie.

iram is standing before Jodie. Bouquet of flowers held in a clenched fist behind his back. In his extended palm, a ribboned ring box. But all she sees is the handle of the *Webley* jutting out from beneath the jacket of his ill-fitting suit. His father's suit.

His smile falters …

The drugs are peaking hard, bringing him back to that moment. He's losing himself, losing the present, losing his mind. He wants to …

"Disappear …" Little Hitler's words are coming from the dark side of the moon.

Jodie's eyes grow wide. She's trying not to scream. Hiram reaches out to touch her and she backs away. "You're the asshole that's been peeking in my windows, aren't you? Snooping through my garbage? Calling and hanging up? What the fuck? What's wrong with you?"

"It's just not fair … there's no one for me … no place for me …" Hitler is sobbing a million miles away.

Hiram searches for the words to make things right. To make her understand. To open his heart. To show her his love. "Jodie, I …," his fishy lips feel bloated and numb. The words choke in his throat.

He wants to tell her that he's loved her since her pigtailed commercial debut for Coppertone and her Disney days. That's he's watched her erotic thriller *The Accused* over four hundred times. He reaches out to touch her shoulder. She cringes, takes a step backwards.

"I'm not like the others …"

Hiram reaches. She screams. He steps forward when—*WHAM!*—a solid kidney punch from behind. Another to the back of his head. Hiram starts to fall when a strong arm grips him and whirls him around. Hiram has a fleeting image of Jodie's enormous bodyguard and overweight driver looming over him before his view is dominated by four gold-and-diamond-blinged knuckles. Smashing his face, his lips, his nose.

"*No one understands ...*"

His wallet is taken. Police are called. Restraining orders are filed.

The name on his driver's license is a fake, but the address is correct. They don't know who he is, but they know where he lives. They know where he's parked his *Airstream*.

"*There's twelve of us, but I feel so alone ...*"

In Hiram's mind, the psychedelic thrumming of the drugs, the discordant harmonics of two grinding realities, the out-of-sync merging of two times—is beating, pulsing, throbbing, in the meat of his brain. A nightmare trip down memory lane.

The judge is not amused. Felony trespass. Felony stalking. Felony attempt to kidnap. Felony peeping. Opium possession. Concealed firearm. Public indecency. Public intoxication.

They know where he lives, but they don't know his name.

"*I just can't do it anymore ...*"

Hiram has no other choice.

A quick elbow to the jaw of his court-appointed attorney. An open-fisted punch to the neck of the court security officer.

Hiram ducks and rolls.

Barrels under the prosecutor's legs. Breaks one of the grim man's knees.

Rolling. Over to the evidence table. The *Webley* back in hand, he scoops up his few belongings, and turns.

A gaggle of police officers, all reaching for their weapons.

Hiram bowls through the pack. Deftly kicking and punching, twisting arms and breaking for the doors. The courtroom is in chaos. People screaming, the judge peeking from behind her desk.

Cops are struggling to take aim, unwilling to fire in such a crowded room. Hiram is breathless, desperate. Making for the double door in the back.

Salvation is in sight, when from the corner of his eye—there she is! Cringing against the seat of her wooden booth! Jodie stares wide-eyed in horror, open mouthed, agape …

Time slows. Becomes an underwater ballet. Hiram reaches nonchalantly out and takes Jodie by the wrist. Pulling her languidly to her feet, he plants a ginger, fish-lipped kiss on her knuckles. Places the small, ribboned box in her palm. Closes her fingers over it.

Gunshots ring out.

"My dear lady," Hiram bows to her, and then he's off—long lanky legs pumping. Through the doors and into the glaring sunlight of Hollywood Boulevard. He doesn't stop until *La La Land* is far behind …

They don't know his name, but they know where he lives.

"*It's too much to bear …*"

Hiram's eyes snap open.

The stale chemical taste of blood and brain fluid—alkaline and harsh, burning stomach acid—thick at the top of his throat. Visions of the past still linger in his mind. Colored dots and geometric patterns dance in his eyes, overlaying the interior of the *Airstream*. Taking form all around him. He's home.

"I'm back," Hiram mutters.

"*I hate who I am …*" young Hitler is holding the *Webley* in cuffed hands. He's placing the barrel in his mouth.

"Nooo!" Hiram lunges, but he's too slow, too late.

Hitler squeezes the trigger.

In slow motion, Hiram watches the hammer rise and fall. Hitler tenses, squeezes shut his eyes. Convulses in expectation of the bullet that never comes.

Click. Nothing happens. An empty shell.

His mother's shell.

(*The suicide shell*)

Hiram bats the gun out of the boy's hands and punches him in the mouth. "The hell's the matter with you?" Hiram sneers. "You're not dying until you tell me where your brothers are … Get up."

Hitler doesn't move.

Hiram hauls him to his feet and cuffs him to the bunk. "We can't stay here. This place is being watched." Paranoid voices are creeping back into Hiram's mind. He swills another chug of absinthe. Straight from the bottle. Un-louched. "Don't move. I just need to get something. Then we'll go see Sadie."

Hiram steps into the *Airstream*'s tiny bathroom and closes the door.

Hitler stares at the door, unsure of what to do. From inside, desperate panting and slapping. Grunts of impatience and pain.

The panting goes on for several minutes before culminating in the retching, choking splash of vomit in the toilet. Hiram emerges, wiping his mouth on his sleeve. In one hand he holds the handgun, in the other a small plastic vial.

"C'mon," orders Hiram, removing Hitler from the bunk post, refastening the cuffs behind the boy's back this time. "Let's go."

On the way out, he grabs the half empty bag of Paradise Chips.

They sneak off into the night, lost to the fog.

Near the *Airstream*, through a shimmering hole in reality, hovering between the boles of the trees, a green eye watches.

They can hear *UberNacht* before they can see it. And they feel it before they can hear it. Deep, rhythmic throbbing. In the bones and the base of the neck. A bass tingling in the pit of the stomach.

The club is inconspicuous (other than the noise)—a small brick building among the derelict factories and old warehouses that now house scores of trendy beatniks, artists and junkies. The club itself is below street level. No windows and little to distinguish the building other than the bouncer at the closed door—a large, over-muscled black man in sweats, a wife-beater and a trench coat. Shaved completely bald. Hiram knows him by the overly ironic handle of 'Mr. Smalls.'

Mr. Smalls sees Hiram and grins. Puts on a barely workable English falsetto that sounds not just strange, but utterly *wrong* coming from the bouncer's mouth. "Well, hello dere, my good man …! And how are we doin' tonight, sir?"

Hiram cracks a smile, returns with, "Well, my dear Mr. Smalls, I do believe we need a drink or twelve!"

The black man laughs good-naturedly, then glances at Hiram's young charge. Hitler seems intent on studying the cracks in the sidewalk. The bouncer's eyes move over to the barely concealed handcuffs—pink fuzz and Dago balls—that Hiram holds behind young Hitler's back.

"Lemme guess, Hiram. No questions?" No fake accent this time. Hiram smiles and maneuvers his captive through the door, down the stairs and into the bar.

Inside, their eardrums are assaulted by the techno-industrial blast of *Nitzer Ebb*.

One step … Twwwwooooo steps …
Getting closer! Getting closer!

With Hitler in tow, Hiram saunters up to the bar.

Sadie is mixing a drink, a blasphemous concoction of Johnny Walker Black Label and Hawaiian fruit punch. When she spies Hiram she drops the drink and leaps over the bar.

"Hey HG! My Hurdy Gurdy Man!" She dives into his arms, clasps her fingers behind his long neck. Wraps her fishnet-stockinged legs around his waist.

She plants a kiss firmly on his gaunt cheek. "You come to sing me songs of love?" Her black hair is dyed a deep crimson, almost purple—matching the stark eyeliner, eye shadow and lipstick painting her otherwise innocent face. Feet laced up in matching purple Doc Martin clodhoppers. She sports a white Oxford shirt and red plaid schoolgirl tie, loose at the collar—the overall effect is to render her abominably cute.

Hiram twirls her around and around, a lighthearted and whimsical faux dance that is uncharacteristic at best. "*Ooh, Sexy Sadie how did you know?*" A singsong whisper in her ear. She's half his age if she's a day. The scent of her shampoo fills him with childhood memories of safety and comfort. She makes him happy. "*The world was waiting just for you-hoo-hoo …?*"

"The latest and the greatest," she smiles. Pecks his cheek and climbs down from his lanky frame. "I got something for ya …" She leaps back over the bar, her short black skirt revealing a tantalizing ribbon of milky inner thigh. Hitler averts his eyes.

Let them believe me,
Let them wonder if I lie ...

From beneath the register, Sadie pulls out a large scrapbook with a macramé cover—the likeness of a young Jodie Foster rendered in knots of colored yarn. Wiping a dry spot on the bar, she opens the book to a random page—a chaotic collage of magazine clippings and newspaper articles. Jodie's face stares out from the pages in all ages, all colors and all resolutions—from blobby ink dots to photo-quality glossies.

"I figured that this might be as close as you're likely to get, so why not make it good ..." Sadie smiles, and Hiram suffers a momentary flashback—blasting his way out of the Los Angeles courtroom, the look of terror and disgust on Jodie's face.

Hitler raises his eyebrows and regards the scrapbook assiduously.

"Er, yes," Hiram closes the book and gently outlines the contours of Jodie's crocheted face with his bony fingers. "I love it ..."

I've got to say that it hurts...
I've got to say that—One step, twwwooooo steps ...
Getting closer! Getting closer!

"Oh!" he does his best to feign nonchalant afterthought. "I have something for you, too ..." He reaches into his pocket.

"Oh, goodie!" Sadie claps her hands together, "Another mix tape? The last one was so—"

"No, actually. It's ..." Hiram places his vial on the bar. The plastic container is half full of viscous white fluid. It's still warm.

"Omigod," Sadie claps her hands over her mouth. "Seriously? Hiram, really?"

"'Kinda drink issat?" a drunk waiting to place his order inquires. "Looks int'restin ...?"

"It's ... sperm," little Hitler says incredulously, as the music switches over to *Nine Inch Nails*.

If I was twice the man I could be,
I'd still be half of what you need ...

"Omigod. I can't believe ... I mean, really ...? Are you sure ...? Hiram?" Sadie is flabbergasted. "I mean I know we talked about it ... you know, as a concept ... but ... I mean ... like, do you think we're ready? I mean ... like, right now?"

Sadie sways and Trent Reznor croons,

Anything you ask you know I'll do ...
But this one act of consecration is what I ask of you ...

Hiram smiles. "Well, if not, there's plenty more where that came from ..." Sadie blushes. Her flushed cheeks in stark contrast to her heavy makeup.

"No ... I mean, yes! I mean ... Let's do it!" She leans over the bar and kisses Hiram firmly on the cheek. She locks her eyes on his, looks deeply into his soul. She shivers, breaks through the ice, "We're gonna be GREAT parents, HG ... You're gonna be an awesome dad ... We're gonna do this right, give our little tyke all the things we never had ..."

Wrap my eyes in bandages,
Confessions I see through ...
I get everything I want,
When I get part of you ...

Again she leaps over the bar. Grabs the plastic vial. Squeezes Hiram in a bear hug (much to the jealous admiration of several voyeuristic onlookers—Sadie is all of a sexy, full-bodied eighteen years. And Hiram, definitely lacking in the looks department, is more than twice her age).

Hiram is her best friend by virtue of being her only friend. '*No, more than that,*' she thinks. '*That's not entirely fair.*' He makes her happy, despite his grim outlook. Despite his self-loathing and self-destructive bent. She sees the Hiram beneath the Hiram—the one who is lonely, in pain. Who only wants to love and to be loved—the one whom she is fairly certain no one else knows exists, least of all Hiram himself.

She plants another kiss on his cheek, and pecks at his ear. "Thank you," she whispers. "Thank you, Hiram. Thank you for taking this chance with me. Thank you for this leap of faith. Thank you for being my friend, my best friend. And thank you, thank you, thank you for not ever once trying to fuck up our friendship with sex. I love you."

Hiram smiles. The expression feels unfamiliar. Uncomfortable.

> *Promise carved in stone ...*
> *Deeper than the sea ...*
> *Devil's flesh and bone ...*
> *Do something for me.*

For the first time Sadie notices Hitler.

His black eye, swollen lip. How his sleeves don't entirely conceal that his wrists are handcuffed behind him. She regards him coolly, "What's with the mustache, bub?"

Hiram laughs. "The gentleman believes he's Hitler." Not exactly a lie. "He's in trouble and I need to keep him out of sight. Keep him from getting hurt ..." Hiram glares at young Hitler, silently daring him to say otherwise. "Keep him from hurting himself."

Hiram turns his eyes imploringly to Sadie, "He needs to lie low for a while ..."

"'Nuff said," Sadie winks. "Say no more ... follow me."

She takes Hiram's hand in her left and Hitler's arm in her right. Leads them through the dark cave of the bar.

Hiram's free hand darts out, deftly grabs a fistful of steaming jalapeño poppers from the plate of an unsuspecting patron at the bar. His mouth is watering. Stomach rumbling. Stuffs them in his pocket for later.

Hiram glances around him as they go—Sadie leading them through the gyrating crowd, towards the back of the techno-industrial cavern. Despite his minutes-old dedication to becoming a daddy, his wandering eyes are drawn to the nubile adolescent bodies all around. *UberNacht* is a virtual meat market of dancing, writhing young flesh, lubricated with alcohol and scented with perfume, tobacco and sweat. There are four kinds of women in the world: those Hiram's slept with, those he hasn't (but would if given the chance), the one he lusts after (*Jodie, oh Jodie, how could thee have forsaken me so?*), and the one he loves—loves enough to father a child with, and loves too much to ever consider seducing ... Sadie. Sexy Sadie.

There are four kinds of women in Hiram's world—and beyond them all there is Mom ... The empty shell in his chamber, the empty vacuum in his soul ... better not to go there, not now, not when important things are afoot, when a mission is at hand. When *The Binge* is ever calling his name ...

Through the kitchen (the smell of burning potato skins and onion rings from the grease trap makes Hiram's mouth water. His mind turns to the confiscated peppers in his pocket, though he knows he is in no condition to keep food down—but soon, maybe. Hopefully. He slows his pace and takes a long pull from his flask, the single malt burns his throat and temporarily postpones the shakes that threaten to wrack his body). Then he continues on down the dark, wet service hallway.

There's a flight of stairs at the end and Sadie leads them down. "There's a sub-basement below the wine cellar," she whispers. "No one ever goes down there. Ever. You'll be safe." She winks at Hitler and he smiles. "Come on, kids. This way ..."

Hiram leans into Hitler's ear. "Don't get too cozy," he hisses. "Your days are still numbered. You've got only as long as it takes me to find your brothers. Then you're dead."

"Don't do me any favors," Hitler replies sardonically.

"Here we are," Sadie, self-professed daughter of the night, disappears into a dark concrete side-room.

A moment later, she pulls a string hanging from the ceiling at the far end of the chamber. Lights a single bare bulb. Rats scurry.

Shelves line the walls, filled with the decades-old remains of forgotten restaurant supplies and empty wine bottles. The deep bass rumble of music from upstairs fills the air. Shakes dust from the ceiling. Muffles their voices.

"You could murder someone down here, and no one would hear it," Sadie laughs. "No one would ever know ... Well, you boys make yourselves at home. I need to visit the little ladies' room." She leans into Hiram's ear, flashes him the vial cupped in her palm. Whispers, "And take care of business before things ... cool down," she flicks his earlobe with her tongue.

She can't wipe the smile from her face.

The moment the door clicks shut, Hiram is on him. Hitler is pinned against the wall, Hiram's hand at his throat. Handcuffed to the shelving now. Hiram punches him in the gut.

"Where are your brothers? I want names and locations. You're going to spill everything you know, or so help me—"

Hitler is wheezing, gasping for breath. "All ... you had ... to do ... was ask. You didn't have to ... hit me ..." He looks Hiram in the eyes. "I'll tell you. Just promise me one thing ..."

"You're in no position to—"

"Just promise me one thing. And I'll tell you everything."

Hiram nods. "I'm listening ..."

"Promise me ..." Hitler coughs and spits a gob of blood onto the floor. "Promise me that when you are finished ... After you've found them all ..."

Hiram sneers.

"Promise me that you'll kill me."

West Searsville Road.

Two and a half hours northwest of New York City. The remote town of Pine Bush. A chill Hudson Valley wind blows through Hiram's tangled hair. The rich smell of manure fills his oversized nostrils. The thrum of a trillion insects fills the air. The stars shine down, a bright canopy blanketing the vast heavens around the pillow of a fat old moon.

Hiram staggers down the unpaved road, heels crunching on gravel and dirt. Sucking opium smoke through the stem of his briarwood pipe—its bowl carved into the likeness of some long-forgotten scowling god or demon. He inhales, holds the cloying smoke deep. Lungs burning, intoxicating explosions creep up his spine.

A stray cat (little more than a kitten, really) approaches from the open field to his left. Hiding in the shadows of the tall trees that loom to the right of the road, Hiram puffs his pipe and shoos the animal.

The cat sniffs at the smoke hanging in the rich Hudson Valley air. Rubs against Hiram's corduroyed legs. Looks up toward the pipe and meows.

Hiram kneels and strokes the feline's back, which arches in appreciation. Hiram smiles. Exhales. Blows smoke in the animal's face.

Whiskers tremble. The cat begins to purr.

Further down the road, a dozen parked cars, headlights off, form a casual line along the unpaved, backwoods lane. Hiram takes a last, long pull on his pipe and puts it out. Slapping the bowl hard against his palm, he dumps the ashes onto the ground. Places the pipe back in his pocket. The stars above seem to grow brighter. Pregnant and ready to explode. Winking and shifting, sending long rays through the night and down to earth. Piercing Hiram's pupils.

Hiram slowly exhales the opium smoke and resumes his drunken, wobbling gait towards the line of cars. The cat follows.

"Boo, kitty," Hiram hisses. "Go on, get outta here …"

Pangs of hunger stab at Hiram's sides. From his pocket he removes a cold, greasy popper. Places the breaded jalapeño gingerly into his mouth. Chews. Swallows. Eats another.

And another.

The congealed grease sticks in his throat. Nauseating, disgusting. Hard swallow. The capsaicin burns his fish-lips, stings the tip of his tongue. His nose is running.

The thought of Sadie, all alone with Hitler in the basement of *UberNacht* won't leave his mind. The deep techno-bass of industrial music miles and miles behind still rings in his ears. The thought of Sadie all alone with Hitler … all alone with a vial of his sperm, his seed …

Such a choice: his life, his future, entwined with the life and future—the unspoken Potential—of another … All now in her fragile hands. Hiram shivers. The Schrödinger lack of control over his destiny is unnerving.

To be or not to be a daddy.

That is the question …

Worms of opium are boring deep holes into his brain. Unleashing streams of memories … Hiram recalls the sharp, commanding voice of his father. Recognizes the timbre of his voice, if not the actual words. His father's voice is metered—it might be poetry, it might be song …

His father's voice, his own …

The opium blurs the edges of memory.

The only thing you need to know about me, Son: I don't need your friendship, I don't need your love …

Who was this? Surely not the father he remembered—the loving man who had been Hiram's only friend, his only confidante, a pillar of encouragement, care and support, before he ...

(Abandoned?)

... before he disappeared. Without a trace. Leaving Hiram with only a dead mother and an empty shell of a life. Lost and without direction. Drowning. Angry.

Helpless ...

The cat paws his leg.

I don't need you ... his father whispers hotly in his ear. It's the drugs speaking, but do they speak the truth?

Never did ...

Where had his father gone?

(Flew the coop?)

Just when young Hiram needed him the most ...

"I said get lost, kitty," Hiram whispers. "Boo ... Shoo ..."

The cat just blinks.

Hiram pulls his *Webley*. Lowers the barrel to just millimeters from the cat's nose. Whiskers twitch. Sandpaper tongue darts out, licks the gunmetal barrel.

"Go away!" Hiram hisses under his breath. The cat just stares, purrs louder. With a sigh, Hiram drops the gun back into his pocket.

Eats another popper. The stale cheese and cold grease coat his tongue. The texture is nauseating.

Hiram grimaces and swallows.

Eats another.

And another ...

West Searsville Road borders an impenetrable field of untamed weeds and huckleberry bramble, ending about a quarter mile off in an unbroken line of trees. Hiram staggers further down the road towards the murmur of distant voices and the glowing embers of burning cigarette butts. The eager kitten follows at his heels.

The cars are closer now.

All of their lights are off. But even under the stars and moonlight, he can read the bumper stickers:

It's hip to see a ship!

My other car is a Flying Saucer!

And simply,

We're all Space Brothers!

An elderly man in a baseball cap sits in a folding lawn chair. *Old Smokey* is emblazoned upon the bill of his hat. A hand-painted placard at his side reads *Take me Home.*

About a dozen skywatchers in all. Men, women and children. One sandy-haired man of indeterminate age (his face entirely obscured by infrared night-vision goggles) stalks the road's edge, pacing back-and-forth, leaning forward and peering into the open field and the tree line beyond.

Lurching down the road, no one has noticed Hiram yet. The jalapeño poppers take a cruel twist in his stomach. His father's voice is still screaming in his head, strange nursery rhymes and the forgotten, febrile music of childhood lessons.

Don't slouch! Finish your Brussels sprouts. Humpty Dumpty had a great fall …

Hallucinations melt into memories: Monsters crawling out of the dark, snatching, grabbing at him—long shadows reaching from the trees and swiping at his head. Hiram cringes as a shadowy hide-behind suddenly lunges—

—the cat brushes his ankles, purring.

Clammy sweat glistens on Hiram's brow.

"I quote Mr. Adolf Hitler," Hiram addresses his feline stalker, "When I say, 'I do not see why man should not be just as cruel as nature ...'" He swings his foot. A wide arc, catching the cat neatly between its front and rear paws. Kicking, lifting and flinging it off into the field with a crash. Down the road, heads turn. The cat lands on its feet and springs back to Hiram's side, purring even louder.

Flannel-shirted men and women—the skywatchers—see him now. They come from all walks of life, but lean towards a crazy, nerdy, unkempt-hair sort of appearance. Some sit, others stand, all focused on the distant tree line, the starry sky. All now turn to regard the lanky man staggering towards them.

All but one. A flannel-shirted Hitler clone sits high up in his own lawn chair, set in the bed of his Chevy pickup. Reposed in his folding throne, perched above the other skywatchers. A wide, disturbing Cheshire grin splits his face, folds his mustache. His eyes remain fixed upon a bright, stationary light parked in the sky at about three o'clock from the waning Moon.

Hiram's eyes follow his gaze. *Venus.*

The planet Venus.

But we'll just keep it between us ... his father's singsong chattering in his brain.

Old Smokey stands up, hand extended. "Pleased to meetcha, friend." The old man shifts his eyes from Hiram, to Venus, and then over to Hitler in his pickup. "Bruce been watchin' that there mothership every night for two weeks now ..." the old man smiles. "We're wondering when she's gonna land."

"It's Venus," Hiram is confused.

The old man frowns. Adjusts his *Old Smokey* hat. "Come again? That thing ain't no star!"

Bruce Hitler clears his throat. "It certainly isn't, Smokes." His voice, relaxed and controlled. He grins, his eyes sliding from the planet to Hiram, taking in the gaunt man from head to toe.

The man in the night-vision goggles saunters over. "You're glowing, man," he says. "Oh, wow …"

"That's Elliot," says Old Smokey, as if this alone would explain the presumption that Hiram was glowing. Hiram *feels* like he is glowing, the opium sends electric shivers up and down his spine.

Elliot pushes the infrared goggles up to his forehead and rubs his eyes. Squints at Hiram. "You here to watch the sky, man? You a skywatcher?" he asks. "You a space brother?"

"Space brothers comin' to take us home," chimes in an elderly lady in a singsong voice. Her gray sweatshirt, finger-painted in blocky letters of alternating primary colors: TAKE US WITH YOU.

The jalapeño poppers take another dangerous flip in Hiram's stomach. Rebelling against digestion, refusing to stay down.

"Go on," says Old Smokey, looking at Hiram but speaking to Bruce. "Tell 'em about the mothership. Tell what's comin' …"

'*What have I stumbled into, here?*' thinks Hiram.

"Tell him about the end times," says Elliot.

"And the Confluences!"

Hiram jerks. Whips around to face the bearer of the young voice who'd mentioned the Confluences. The boy is no older than nine, his shirt emblazoned in the same handcrafted, finger-painted style as his mother's:

WE BELIEVE!

'*The Confluences!*' thinks Hiram, a surge of acrid jalapeño mush rising and burning the back of his throat. It was the Confluences—strange and powerful tears in the fabric of reality, portals between this world and those below and above—that primarily concerned the *Office of Independent Research and Analysis*. These Confluences were the reason that the OIRA paid Hiram so dearly (in more than just money—the elusive organization unstintingly catered to the man's many strange tastes and exotic vices) to visit these sites. And to destroy whatever came through them.

Ground Zero was the most recent Confluence in OIRA records. The Office had been monitoring New York City's downtown closely since that tragic 9/11 morning. The morning when the very fabric of Reality had been torn asunder by the fuel-filled jet planes and raging infernos, the tumbling tons of concrete—by the unprecedented act of blind hate, and the deaths of untold innocents. The Confluence marked a scar, an open wound, from which the world would not heal anytime soon.

The little he knew about his current mission—the twelve renegade Hitlers—was the scant details that his handler, the elusive Mrs. Bothwell, had told him. In Cyrillic-encrypted e-mails as *Gashleycrumb* (the OIRA powers that be had felt it wise to take every possible precaution in the wake of what they called "The Foster Incident" to maintain as many degrees of separation between the organization and unpredictable Agent Grange as possible, at least until the fallout of his most recent indiscretion blew over). Mrs. Bothwell had sent him the bare essentials needed to set him on a path of murder and cover-up. A mission of sterilization, of tying loose ends.

According to Mrs. Bothwell, the Hitlers had emerged from the rubble of Ground Zero on that fateful September morning. Whether or not they had actually come through the newly opened Confluence, stepped out of the Abyss, was uncertain. But Hiram didn't think so. He'd encountered malevolent denizens of The Abyss before (*The Abyss*—a catch-all name for those countless pocket dimensions thriving in parasitic contact with our own Reality. Ever poking and prodding, sucking life and injecting poison—mushrooming off the underside of the world like so many unchecked warts and boils). Or at least he thought he'd encountered them—the drugs played funny games with the memory, the absinthe told its own story, *The Binge* created its own reality. And the very nature of the Abyss defied imprinting itself on the organic hard drive of the brain ...

Things better left forgotten, all too often were ...

Hiram seemed to recall a recent battle … cloudy details bubbling to the surface of his drug-addled memory. Enormous tentacles squeezing, pulling … a lungful of inky brine … a giant, myopic, fishy eye, and row upon endless row of barbed teeth … fighting under the water (was it the Greek Isles? That seemed somehow right), fighting with his knife and his hands … it had been close, but Hiram had prevailed, prevailed as he always had against the monsters of the Abyss … or had it all just been a dream? Were the drugs playing games with his memory? Screwing with his subconscious? Fucking with his waking mind? Certainly, it *seemed* like another life … like a film fantasy … in truth, how *could* it be real? How could any of it be real? The monsters of the Abyss …?

And yet, somehow *this* was different … this mission: not monsters, but boys … teens … innocent children … Innocent?

(*You can't trust them*, Gashleycrumb warned. *They're devious. Intelligent. Evil … And older, the clones don't age as quickly as we do …*)

Crazies cloned from Hitler's DNA. (Hiram was sure now that they had *not* come from the Abyss, just as he is suddenly doubtful of the very *reality* of the Abyss … unsure, untrusting of his own memory, his own mind) … Cloned from a monster. An all-too-*human* monster, to be sure. But human just the same …

A sudden light over the tree line catches Hiram's eye, startles him from the brain-traps of his opium-altered introspection. All the skywatchers are now facing him, their backs to the trees. Only Hiram sees the light. It slowly rises—small, iridescent, pulsating. It seems to defy gravity. Wavering over the treetops, swaying gently, as if caught in a breeze, first to the left, then to the right. Shimmering, as if from the bottom of a deep pool.

Hitler is still speaking.

"… if only you'd seen the things that I've seen down there: secret train cars on secret tracks, deep beneath Grand Central Station.

Stockade boxcars customized with human shackles. Cattle cars and camps ready and waiting for hundreds of thousands ... If only you knew the things that I know: The end times aren't coming, they're here! The second holocaust is upon us. *The Cascade* has been unleashed ... A new era of fear and suffering is upon us ... But the chosen few, those *in the know*," Hitler smiles, extending his arms to the skywatchers and to the sky in rapt attention all around. "The space brothers are coming to take us home ..."

"Back to the stars, man," says Elliot.

"Back to the Garden ..."

"Well, that's hippie-dippy dandy," says Hiram, eyes never leaving the light hovering over the trees. Growing brighter, closer. Something in the back of his mind warns him to stop wasting time, to hurry up and get the job done. "But what's that you were saying about a Confluence?"

"When the Towers came down," says Bruce, "That's when a hole was ripped in the ass end of New York City ..."

The voice in Hiram's head is strong now, urging him to hurry. His roiling stomach seconds the motion. The light is drawing closer, ever closer. Hiram is transfixed. He doesn't know how he knows it, but his time here is running out. "Keep going," he says. "You know this, how?"

"A tear in the underbelly of the world," Hitler smiles, "Deep underground where secret things were already in motion. We lived there, my brothers and I. We saw things. Evil things, yes, but they were the evils of men. Of scientists and politicians, people too smart and too greedy for their own good. But when the buildings fell and the Confluence ripped open ..."

The voice in Hiram's head is screaming now. His father's voice. Pressing him to get his ass moving. Stop thinking. Do his job. Angry reprimands mixed with childhood bedtime stories.

This is no time for play! This is no time for fun! This is no time for games! There is work to be done! and *I never loved you ... I never needed you ...!*

('No,' thinks Hiram. 'That's the drugs talking. Daddy *did* love me …')

I never wanted you …

(He DID.)

"The things that came through," Hitler lowers his voice. "They were terrifying. All we could do was run. Run, and try to dig our way out of the smoking rubble. While behind us, we could see only …"

Your mother pulled the trigger. But it should've been you, Hiram. It should've been you. But you weren't man enough to do it. Never were, never will be. You're just an empty shell of a man …

A disappointment …

The drugs are really taking hold. Hitler is still speaking, but all Hiram hears is his father, screaming over and over again, *Do it! Do it! Do it!*

"… it had started and there was no stopping it. The Cascade—"

BLAM!

The *Webley* is smoking in Hiram's shaking hand.

Hitler is dead.

There is no sound but the wind. Then a strange music starts. Faint at first, echoing in the depths of Hiram's mind, taking root between his ears in the wake of the gunshot. A chorus of gasps and moans, a choir of tears, edged with the frantic cacophony of hysteria and disbelief …

The light draws closer. Only Hiram sees it.

A luminous, rectangular box. All windows and light. Several small forms stand in silhouette, featureless and diminutive, shaking their oversize egg-shaped heads. Accusing, condemning in unearthly silence. For a frozen moment they regard Hiram sadly. And then, as strangely as it had appeared, the craft is gone—leaving Hiram alone with the wind and the stars, the dead and the living.

The gun in his hand hangs at his side. He stares at the empty star-filled space the craft has left in its wake.

Go on, sniggers his father. *Stare at the stars. But don't think that they're lining up for you. They've got better things to do …*

In the slow-motion riot of reaction to his cold-blooded shooting, Hiram half expects demons and saucers to come screaming out of the woods, tentacles to erupt from the trees, fiery fissures to open in the ground and swallow him whole … but nothing.

Silence.

People in shock, sobbing to themselves, frozen in place. The insects slowly resume their chatter. And then one of the skywatchers begins to shriek …

Sharp pangs of hunger bite at his sides. Drugs and alcohol and acid and bile are eating away at the lining of his stomach. Nerves and anxiety and cold-blooded remorse gnaw at his gut. Gnawing at his damned soul—the possibility of his best and only friend bearing his demon child is suddenly too much for him. Hiram turns and vomits. Blood and bile. Jalapeño poppers—chewed but not digested—splatter on West Searsville Road. Forever staining the place. Mixing with the blood of Bruce Hitler.

Hiram staggers off. The shell-shocked UFO watchers just stare. And the unfathomable actions of the past sixty seconds are lost to the silent night and the crickets.

Cold-blooded murders don't go unnoticed. But they do go unsolved.

In the years to follow—though they never knew his name, his motives or his nature—the skywatchers would come to refer to Hiram as *The Pine Bush Phantom* and the *Searsville Stalker*. A vision of alien evil and ghostly malice that would appear on nights of the waning moon when Venus was at three o'clock to take a life. Take a life and then vanish … mysteriously and without a word. Leaving only death and taking only his cat.

Fourth little Hitler, only wants to get high.

Mr. Smalls just smiles as the haggard, disheveled man cuts to the front of his line. The bouncer knows better than to get between Hiram and *UberNacht* when the gaunt man looks like he does. He's seen Hiram at his worst—and tonight Hiram seems to have beaten his own personal best for decrepitude. And by quite a long shot …

'Even on the best of days, the man is a pill,' thinks Mr. Smalls. 'And on a night like tonight, looking like he does, old Hiram is bound to be a veritable fart in church.'

Hiram pushes his way through the crowded, slow-motion strobe of the dance floor, making for the back of the bar. Trench coat trailing, wild-eyed and tangled hair. Before him, the mosh pit ceases its violent thrashing, the crowd parts to let him pass. A Red Sea of gyrating, perfumed and sweating young bodies.

Hiram marches forward, staring at the illuminated screen of his iPhone. The one piece of technology that his OIRA handlers wouldn't let Hiram the technophobe go without. Frowning at the latest message from Gashleycrumb:

> 26 Industrial St. 3rd Floor.
> His name is Livingstone. Good luck.
> —Gashleycrumb

Livingstone Hitler—Little Hitler number four.

Hiram is suddenly aware of the nubile crowd all around him. A hangnail picks at the back of his brain, hairs bristle on the back of his neck. Again that unmistakable feeling of being watched …

He spares a quick glance backwards into the cavernous club. The dancers are dancing, the moshers are moshing—slinky girls are slinking. And there, in the corner, a long shadow in the mirrored wall, silhouetted in strobe, looking his way and then gone.

Hiram spares another moment, his head heavy and drunk with the drugs and the music and the lights, but the figure doesn't return. Hiram frowns, then scuttles through the back door, down the stairs, and into the abandoned supply room.

No sooner has he opened the door when Sadie is upon him.

"Did you really threaten him with a gun!" she demands, indicating the little Hitler handcuffed in the corner. Hitler refuses to meet his glaring eyes. "What in the world were you *thinking*?" Sadie exclaims.

"What did he say to you—"

"His *name* is Edsel," Sadie interrupts. "And he didn't *say* anything. I *asked* him and he *told* me."

'*And he just signed his own death warrant,*' thinks Hiram. '*And sooner, rather than later.*'

"I just ... I—"

"Never mind that," Sadie can barely conceal the smile on her face. She can't unglue her eyes from Hiram's. She is studying every inch of him. Every wrinkle, every crooked feature of his face, every dark shadow lurking in his eyes. There is not a portion of his tired flesh that does not bear a scar. "It doesn't matter what happened. I just want you to be nicer to him in the future, Hiram."

She's grinning now from ear to ear. "I want you to be *nice* ..." She plants a kiss on his cheek and slips something hard into the palm of his hand. Closes his fingers over it. "For you," she whispers hotly in his ear. "For you, my nice, nice man ..."

Her eyes, expectant. Imploring.

In his palm, the glass vial. Empty and cold.

She's taking him all in, every ugly inch of him. Wrapping his haggard features in ribbons and bows, hiding them in the Christmas closet of her mind, to unwrap and explore later. Savoring every expression, cherishing every reflected emotion in the deep pupils of his dark eyes. Perhaps imagining the features of her future child ... *Their* child ...

Hiram holds her gift up to his face, just inches from his twisted nose. Licks his chalky lips. Cold drug-sweat dampens his clothes, shivers walk up and down his spine. A dank, alkaline odor hovers around his armpits. He studies the empty vial, looking deep into the glass for any omen of the future, acknowledgement of things to come.

"Thank you, Sadie," he's at a loss for words. "I ..."

Hiram drops his hand to his side, stuffs the vial into his coat pocket. His fingers encounter something unexpected—not the cold steel of his *Webley*, not the leftover grease and crumbs of jalapeño poppers. Something warm. Furry.

Alive.

"I ... I've got something for you, too, Sadie," Hiram makes an awkward attempt at a smile, but his face is unpracticed and unwilling to comply. "To keep you company until, well, until ... you know ..." He yanks the startled cat from his pocket and plops it into Sadie's arms.

"His name is Boo," Hiram stammers. "He needs a home ..." The cat is purring. Sadie is ecstatic. Even Edsel Hitler can't contain his smile.

"Oh, Hiram! He's adorable! I love him! Where did you ... No, don't tell me. I don't think I want to know ..." She buries her face in the Calico's unruly fur, smothers it in coos and motherly kisses.

Hiram backs towards the door. He has a date: *Livingstone. 26 Industrial St. 3rd Floor—Hitler number four.*

Hiram turns to leave. Sadie turns to her man. Still cuddling the cat, she uses her sleeve to wipe blood from a long scratch on Hiram's brow, licks her fingers to clean a smudge of dirt from his cheek. "You're a good man, Hiram. And you're gonna be a good father," she frowns. "But you gotta take care of yourself. I'm worried that you seem to be on a dangerous path—"

"I always take care of myself." Hiram can feel the beast stretching its claws in the deeper recesses of his sorry excuse for a soul. The drugs are unfurling their sails, *The Binge* is stirring and calling his name. The Mission is pushing and pulling.

Sadie's eyes are boring into him. He tries to turn away, but she holds him fast.

He has to go. Has to go now.

"Not out there," Sadie hands the kitten to Hitler, then kisses Hiram's temple. "I know you always take care of yourself out there." She taps his forehead. "Promise me you'll take care of yourself in here …"

The man peeking out through the narrow opening of the chain-locked apartment door is barely even recognizable as Hitler. Stained sweatpants and a bathrobe over a tie-dyed shirt. Long unkempt hair and a scruff of patchy week-old beard. Bare feet and thick, fungal toenails. His true nature betrayed only by the distinct mustache on his upper lip. He reeks of hemp and patchouli.

Hiram smirks and kicks in the door, breaking the chain.

Inside the apartment is a makeshift laboratory. Bubbling beakers and test tubes. Laptop computers sit haphazardly on edges of desks, on the arms of a ratty old couch. Piles of pills, bundles of hypodermic needles, mountains of strange powders, sheets of paper blotters, microscopes and scales litter the room. In the corner, balanced precariously on a stained mattress, sits a large, ornate glass bong. The apartment stinks of body odor and stale smoke, animal urine and bitter chemicals

"Dr. Livingstone, I presume?" Hiram steps inside and draws his gun. Staring down the barrel of the *Webley*, the degenerate Hitler backs away, trips and lands on the mattress. Bong water spills, staining the mattress a deep brown and filling the room with an overpowering swampy stench.

"Oh, man … don't … please don't …" the psychedelic urchin begs as Hiram closes the door behind him. Levels the gun. Cocks the hammer.

"C'mon, man …" Hitler pleads. "Let's work this out …"

"Nice meth lab you've got here," Hiram's tone is disapproving.

"Meth lab!" Hitler is suddenly indignant. "Meth lab? This is a designer studio, man!"

Keeping the gun trained on Hitler, Hiram gazes around the dingy apartment. Colorful liquids stream through lengths of glass tubing, strangely-colored toads peep out from glass terrariums. In a rusty cage in the corner of the room, a small chimpanzee is wearing a tie-dyed diaper and a hippie headband. Smoking a cigarette. The chimp slowly raises one hand. Extends two fingers.

Waves the *Peace!* sign at Hiram. Takes a long drag on his smoke.

"Okay. You've got thirty seconds," Hiram states flatly. "What's with the monkey? Start talking."

Hitler opens his mouth to speak, but no sound escapes. He licks his lips, tries again, still can't find the words. Clears his throat.

"Oh god. You're going to kill me, aren't you?"

"Yes."

The chimp begins to hoot and holler, clapping its hands. Cigarette butt dangling from its lip.

"How about … how about a last cigarette?" Hitler implores. "That would be okay, wouldn't it? You wouldn't deprive a guy one last toke, wouldja?" The young man rises to his knees and slowly crawls to an equipment-laden table. All the while holding his palms out towards Hiram, as if to ward off any bullets or violent ideas.

Hitler rifles through the piles of junk on the table—empty beer bottles and used syringes, overflowing ashtrays and browning banana peels. "Smokes ... smokes ... who's got the smokes?" Empty Bic butane lighters, take-out fast-food cartons, plastic film canisters, pill bottles, rolling papers and glass pipes. But no cigarettes.

"For the love of god," Hitler mumbles, exasperated. "My kingdom for a cancer stick ..."

"Time's up," Hiram levels the *Webley*.

"Wait! Please, wait ..." begs Hitler. "There's gotta be a cigarette here somewhere ..." he desperately digs through the junk. "Or better yet ..." his eyes light up. Hiram can almost see the metaphoric lightbulb shimmering above his head. Livingstone Hitler looks at Hiram and smiles, "Better yet ...

"Wanna get high?"

"To get really high is to *forget* yourself," Hitler is saying. Arms outstretched, hands held high, fingers splayed, jerky motions to punctuate his points. He and Hiram are sitting on the floor. Livingstone in a comfortable full lotus and Hiram with his lanky knees pulled up to his chest. A bulbous hookah sits between them, hashish and hash oil smoldering in the bowl. Two long hoses trail out from the thing—one mouthpiece gripped in Hitler's hand, the other in Hiram's. "And to forget *yourself* is to finally *see everything else*. And to see everything else is to *become* an understanding molecule in evolution, a conscious tool of the universe. That's what my man Jerry Garcia said ..."

Hiram is staring at his hands. They seem too large, like cartoon hands. The flesh seems to be breathing, rising and falling. Myriad patterns twist and writhe, mingling with the hairs and folds of his skin.

Adolf Hitler was fascinated by hands. True fact. Kept a book of pictures and drawings of the hands of famous people. Bragged that his own hands were nearly identical to those of his hero, Frederick the Great.

"Way I see it, man, psychedelic drugs are not a vacation *from* reality, they're a vacation *to* reality."

Adolf Hitler was also a speed freak. True fact.

The slow bass of *The Grateful Dead* jamming a Dylan tune emanates from the speakers of Hitler's stereo system, punctuated by the musical croaking of Livingstone's psychoactive toads. Blue smoke hangs in the air.

> *He woke up, the room was bare, he didn't see her anywhere,*
> *He told himself he didn't care, pushed the window open wide …*

The chimpanzee has been freed from its cage. Now sitting comfortably, legs crossed, on the couch. Smoking a roach through a pair of tweezers. Taking it all in. Mellow and grooving to the music.

Digging the vibe. Loving the atmosphere.

> *Felt an emptiness inside to which he just could not relate,*
> *Brought on by a simple twist of fate …*

"Does he have a name?" Hiram nods at the chimp.

"I just call him The Doctor," Hitler shrugs.

"What about the frogs?"

"They don't have names."

"No, I mean, what are they? What for?" Hiram's mind is a whirlpool, his thoughts spiraling down into his subconscious. It's getting harder to formulate ideas, difficult to construct sentences. "What's their deal?"

"*Bufo alvarius*, man. Sonoran Desert Toads. Their secretions are one of the most psychoactive substances known to man."

"What do you … lick them?" Hiram takes another toke from the hookah and chases it with a long pull from his Budweiser tallboy. The *Webley* is lying on the floor at Hiram's feet. Out-of-hand, but within easy reach.

"No man, licking toads is a myth … you gotta milk them."

"Huh." Hiram is feeling the deep effects of the hashish. Visions of milking frogs dance through his brain. He shakes his head. "How?"

"You milk the venom from the toad's parotoid glands, man. But even then, you can't just lick it. It's poison. Kill a guy your size in three minutes flat. You've gotta dry it and smoke it."

Hitler holds up a small plastic baggie filled with a thick yellow powder. "Whaddaya say?"

Hiram frowns. Considers. All good sense is lost in the foggy dead-end maze of his mind, better judgment is drowning in the muck of his brain, escaping through his ears. He seems to recall a job in the not-too-distant past—*a mission*. All blood and violence, guns blazing and hellfire, grappling with a thousand-eyed Abysmal, while all around them frogs rained down from the sky. Memory or delusion? Is there even a difference, anymore?

"All right," Hiram says, "Fire it up."

"It's like Abby Hoffman said, man. Drugs are just a tool to turn us into what we are supposed to be. If you've ever felt the rising panic of '*Did I overdo it? Did I take too much?*' Then, shit man, you obviously haven't taken enough …" Hitler's pupils are enormous. Black holes filled with countless stars.

Hitler's words take physical shape, emerging from his mouth, rolling off his tongue. The words are imbued with color, smell and sound, but are losing their meaning. Stringing together in long trains, but lacking cohesion … Mad Libs of the undermind … Hiram swallows hard, tries to keep focused.

"What you don't understand you can make mean anything," Hitler postures. "Einstein said that, he said, 'Since the initial publication of the charged electromagnetic spectrum, humans have learned that what they can touch, smell, see, and hear … is less than one millionth of reality. Once you can accept that the universe is matter expanding into nothing, wearing stripes with plaid comes easy.' Crazy, right?"

Hiram clears his throat. "Adolf Hitler said that anyone who sees and paints a sky green and fields blue ought to be sterilized." He's trying to provoke the young Hitler. Trying to get this train back on its tracks. "What do say to that, my dear Livingstone?"

Hitler is nonplussed. "'Great liars are also great magicians.' Hitler also said that. And we chemists and pharmacologists are the greatest magicians of them all. We're modern-day psychedelic Alchemists, man! The chance of going insane on drugs is far less likely than going insane without them. It's like they say: They can get it out of your blood, but they can't get it outta your brain ..."

Hitler is laying out long lines of a fine pink powder on a handheld mirror. Takes a pair of glass straws from his shirt pocket and hands one to Hiram. "'I don't do drugs, I am drugs.' Salvador Dali." He holds the mirror under Hiram's enormous nose. "This is designer stuff, man. My latest invention. Like nothing that's come before. It'll take you past the farthest galaxies, to the Octopus's Garden on the ocean's floor. It'll blow your socks off."

Hiram leans forward. His nostrils are so cavernous that he has to pinch his nose to hold the straw. But before he can inhale the fine powder he stops, suddenly hypnotized by the face staring back at him. Eyes wide and bloodshot, exploded pupils, bulbous witch-nose, wild knotted hair—Hiram doesn't recognize his own reflection. Sallow complexion, dark half-moons under his eyes. His lips are dry and cracked. Teeth crooked and yellow. Ratty, uneven patches of unshaven scruff mar his face, cover his bony chin. He looks like death warmed over. '*Who is this sad man?*' he thinks. '*This omen of tragic despair? This wraith who looks as if he hasn't eaten in days, weeks, years?*' The ghostly countenance shimmers, draws closer ... Closer still ...

With a sharp, audible report the glass straw hits the mirror. *WHACK!* A thin crack divides Hiram's lachrymose face in half—two sides out of sync. Time slows down. One side of Hiram now seems lost in shadow, the other bathed in light. There's a splash as a drop of blood falls to the broken mirror, mixing with the pink powder. Clotting into paste. Hiram watches, fascinated, as three more drops of blood fall upward. Dripping from the end of the straw in the mirror-vision's nose, deep within the glass, falling up, up to the mirror's surface. Hiram is lost in the blood and glass, lost in the surreal reflection ...

From the stereo, Leonard Cohen's serenade is deep, sultry, apropos:

There is a crack ... There is a crack, in everything,
That's how the light gets in ...

Hitler turns to the radio. "Far out, man. Synchronicity. Only when you're tripping ..."

He withdraws the cracked mirror from under Hiram's bleeding nose. "No problem man, the dust didn't spill. Wanna try it again? You still got one good nostril ... Whaddaya say? Hit me baby, one more time? One toke over the line, bro ...?"

"Why does everything that feels so good have to hurt so much?" Hiram wipes blood onto the white-starched ruffle of his sleeve. Switches the glass straw to his other nostril. Leans forward and vacuums pink dust into his lungs.

The drugs explode in his brain, clearing his sinuses, sending bolts of electricity down his spine. Tingling his toes. Hiram can feel his fingernails floating at the ends of his fingers, electric pulsing in the crowns of his teeth, sparks of energy riding down his long eyelashes and through his tangled hair. The room around him has shifted into hyper-reality: walls shimmer and glow, music flows in audible rainbows from the throbbing, gyrating stereo speakers. The air around him feels cool on his cheeks, tastes clean on his tongue. Motes of dust hang languidly before his eyes, entire galaxies suspended in the space between him and Hitler.

The angles and lines where the walls meet the ceiling and the floor begin to bend and twist, stretching onward to infinity, ceasing to make sense and yet screaming wordless poignancy and sage, architectural wisdom.

What is a room? The floor, walls and ceiling? Or the space contained within? Can one exist without the other?

Hiram's mind is sharp, his eyes darting. His senses, hyper-aware.

"Feelin' better? That's the stuff, eh? Happy trails and good vibes!" Hitler gives his own glass straw a salutatory flick, raises the mirror to his nose and takes a snort. "Yowza!"

Hiram raises his hands in front of his eyes. Sure enough, they are glowing, leaving rainbow trails in the air. Wiggles his fingers and crystalline sparks emanate from the tips. He has the sudden impression that he can see out of each of his eyes individually, not double vision, but two distinct and separate movies relayed simultaneously to his brain. The world is unfolding all around him, revealing atavistic secrets and indefinable mysteries.

"Check this out," Hitler indicates a petri dish on his desk. "Ever done a psychedelic thumbprint?"

Hiram shakes his head. In the dish, a walnut-sized block of indigo crystal. Ominous and silent, it practically explodes with lascivious, psychedelic mischief. "What *is* that?"

"It's LSD in pure crystal form," Hitler grins. "You press your thumb against the face of the crystal. Absorb it through your skin and get the most powerful dose humanly possible. Ten thousand hits in the blink of an eye. The trip can last for days. Sometimes even weeks. It's a religious experience. More than a religious experience. Nothing else even comes close. Except maybe *this* …" Livingstone whispers conspiratorially. "Wanna see something *really* special?"

He sidesteps over to his workbench. Beakers bubble, a laptop computer displays slowly rotating polygonal models of molecules. Livingstone picks up a small, black felt box of the sort that might hold an engagement ring, or a pair of expensive cuff links.

He flips open the box and holds it out for Hiram to see. Nestled in the soft fabric is a pill. Shiny and blue, almost iridescent, it's the largest pill Hiram has ever seen. Etched onto its surface is the beveled letter,

"What is it?" Hiram's eyes are locked on the pill. "Heroin?"

Hitler laughs. "Not heroin, not by a long shot. No man, this is IT! *The Big H*. Specially designed for my boss. The ultimate experience, man, it'll reveal the ultimate truth, open doorways to other places, close doors to others ..."

"What's in it?"

"You don't wanna KNOW what's in this ... What's in it? The TRUTH, man!! The trooth, da whole trooth, and nuttin' but da TROOTH! The end-all, be-all ... The *Confluence*, man!" Hitler's eyes take on a faraway look. "To start with, DMT harvested from the brains of human embryos on the forty-ninth day of the first trimester—the moment that the pineal gland opens its godly eye and squirts life into the biology of the brain, man. That's just for starters ..." he grins. "Your appetite whet yet? Hows about extracted hormones of psychedelic jellyfish harvested from the ocean's floor at the deepest part of the Mariana Trench? Hows about a pure tincture of Ayahuasca? *Ergot Prime* liberated from the secret vaults of *Operation Mindfuck* below Area 51? Amino lysergic acids recovered from the Titicaca meteor crash in Peru? Huh? How's that for *starters* ...?

The chimp claps its hands, begins jumping up and down on the couch. The tie-dyed headband brings out the blue in his eyes. The animal opens its mouth, baring its teeth and revealing two tabs of blotter acid. Ink runs from the paper, staining the pink skin of its tongue.

"The boss calls it the Final Solution, which I personally find a bit distasteful ..."

Hiram doesn't miss a beat. Keeping Hitler's eyes locked on his own, his long fingers snake out across the floor. Silently take hold of his gun. "Who's your boss?" Hiram asks, the *Webley* an old friend in his steel grip.

"My boss? My boss is the jolly green giant, man ... the one-eyed pea ..."

Hiram can feel the old familiar meanness creeping up his spine. Cold, hard light fills the periphery of his vision. His gun, an extension of his arm.

"What's the Big H for, Livingstone?"

"It's the ultimate in mind expansion. Take you to the next level. Green Dude conceived it, but *I* designed it ..." Hitler's voice trails off. His eyes suddenly glaze over. Hiram notes an almost imperceptible expansion of his pupils.

"What for?" Hiram's voice is flat, his eyes like chiseled granite.

"He needs it to fulfill his plans," Livingstone's voice suddenly becomes monotone, his words suddenly soft around the edges. Rote. Hiram recognizes a post-hypnotic suggestion when he sees one. "There's a great war coming. Soon the Cascade will be revealed. But before that there're plans to be made ... Plans and preparations ... The Green One, *La Fée Verte*, will have a seat at the left hand ... but only if he can first vanquish the White Knight, the Foe of the Abyss, the Holy Warrior ..."

"Who?"

"Some clown named Hiram."

Hiram clenches the inside of his cheek between angry teeth. His finger trembles on the trigger of the *Webley*. "And the pill?"

"... should be taken just before the ultimate confrontation. A secret weapon. To ensure the defeat of his greatest enemy."

'*What is this?*' Hiram thinks. '*For whom is the message intended? Is this a clue? Or a trap?*'

Life seems to bleed back into Livingstone. His eyes widen in fear, his lips begin to tremble. "Oh my," he squeaks, "I've said too much, haven't I?"

BLAM!

Acrid blue smoke rises from the *Webley*'s gunmetal barrel, burning Hiram's bloody nostril and stinging his dilated eyes. The chimpanzee laughs and applauds.

Livingstone Hitler crumples to the floor. His pupils shrink to pinpoints and his eyes grow wide as he dies, kneeling in an expanding pool of blood.

'*Curiouser and curiouser …*' Hiram wonders. '*H for Hitler? Or H for Hiram? Who shall get the lucky pill? Door prize or booby prize? Bane or boon? Disaster or jackpot?*'

The Big H. The Final Solution.

The stereo adds its own two cents:

> *One pill makes you larger …*
> *And one pill, makes you small …*

Hiram or Hitler? Hitler or Hiram?

Hiram picks up the pill, holds it up in front of his eyes, just past the end of his abused nose. The Big H, the Final Solution … Hitler's power pop.

'*Flip the coin?*' he thinks. '*Bottoms up? Down the hatch? Buy a ticket, take a ride? Taste the rainbow?*'

Maybe. Yes, probably, in fact. But not yet. He snaps the pillbox shut and drops it into the deep pocket of his coat. He knows he'll be swallowing that pharmaceutical Pandora's Box at some point. But for now … for now there are other options. Always other options.

Hiram quickly surveys the tables and shelves, Hitler's cluttered workbench. Working fast, sure that the neighbors have heard the gunshot. Called the cops.

Hiram stuffs his pockets with exotic drugs: handfuls of strange-smelling joints—cigs rolled with bizarre, hybridized, genetically manipulated tropical plants, psychotropic truffles and lichen, seeds and entheogens … syringes filled with phosphorescent, viscous opiates of all colors … pills of all shapes and sizes … and …

The stereo is screaming:

> *Feed your head …! Feed your head …!*

There's no avoiding it. The Thumbprint is beckoning, calling his name, calling his thumbs, as it were. Hiram sighs. There's no use fighting it. No way to ignore it.

He takes a deep breath and presses both thumbs against the dangerous lump of crystallized indigo ergot.

There's a jackrabbit surge of energy up his arms, locking his elbows akimbo and tickling his funny bones. The stiffness of his collar bones melts away. The room takes on an electric blue tinge, fleeting shadows whisper at the periphery of his vision. An oceanic rush fills his ears, throwing him off balance. There's a pulsating in the base of the neck, where the spine meets the skull. The cradle of the soul, rocking gently in its treetop, falls and shatters on the forest floor. Hiram's inner child cries and wails, screaming bloody and broken in the dark night of his psyche.

The chimp's high-pitched *Hoo hoo, haa haa* fills the air.

"My ... god ..." Hiram holds his hands to his ears, tries to keep his brains on the inside. Multicolored rainbow serpents are streaming in and out of the floorboards. Desperate visions of peering eyes, laughing faces and gnashing teeth are painting themselves on the atavistic cave walls inside his skull.

His head feels as if it's inflating like a balloon, he's afraid it might pop. Hiram sticks his thumbs in his mouth, massaging the insides of his cheeks ... and then realizes what he's doing: Those were the same two thumbs that he'd just pressed to the sides of the electric acid crystal ... weren't they?

Did that happen yet?

Or was it about to?

Time is folding in on itself, refusing to make sense.

Hiram turns for the door, only to find himself already running for it. Hand already on the knob, he's already out in the hall, while back in the apartment his foot comes down hard on one of the Doctor's discarded banana peels ...

Comes down hard and slides …

Time is sliding …

Going down fast …

Hiram is falling, falling …

The Binge … The Binge is in full tilt, and of record proportions. This just may be the end-all be-all for dear old Hiram. It's the loop-de-loop … The loop-de-loop, and long fall …

But he'll pull out just before hitting rock bottom. He always does …

But for now, *The Binge*.

But never like this before … This is new.

Different. Dangerous.

A new high, a new low …

And now …

Now things are getting weird …

Fifth little Hitler, all juiced up . . .

Fast, ancient drums pound in his head. Beating prehistoric rhythms on the insides of his eardrums, along the canals of his ears, and smashing against medulla oblongata and cerebral cortex. A primeval soundtrack to his murderous, Hitler-killing spree.

The sour smells of sweat and adrenaline invade his nose.

Just moments ago: clanging metal and heavy grunting—the sounds of exertion and slamming weights. Then the muffled thuds of dumbbells dropped in surprise, hitting the foam floor.

And now only silence.

Silence, and deadly anticipation.

Adolf Hitler had absolutely no interest in physical fitness. Never exercised. Never played any sports. True fact.

Adolf Hitler didn't work out. But Bruno Hitler did—to a fault.

Hiram stares down the barrel of the *Webley*, one eye squinting, the other focused on his target. Bruno lies prone on the weight bench. Rivulets of sweat streak his furrowed brow. His over-muscled arms, thick as tree trunks and popping with veins, suspend an impossibly heavy barbell in mid-press above his ripped, six-pack abs. His eyes are on Hiram.

All eyes are on Hiram.

The stink of drugs and toxic sweat rises from Hiram's armpits, mixing with the last remnants of his patchouli cologne.

Adolf Hitler refused to use any sort of cologne or scent on his body. True fact.

Hiram's stomach rumbles. Turning on itself, rebelling against a diet of psychedelics and alcohol. Beginning the first stages of

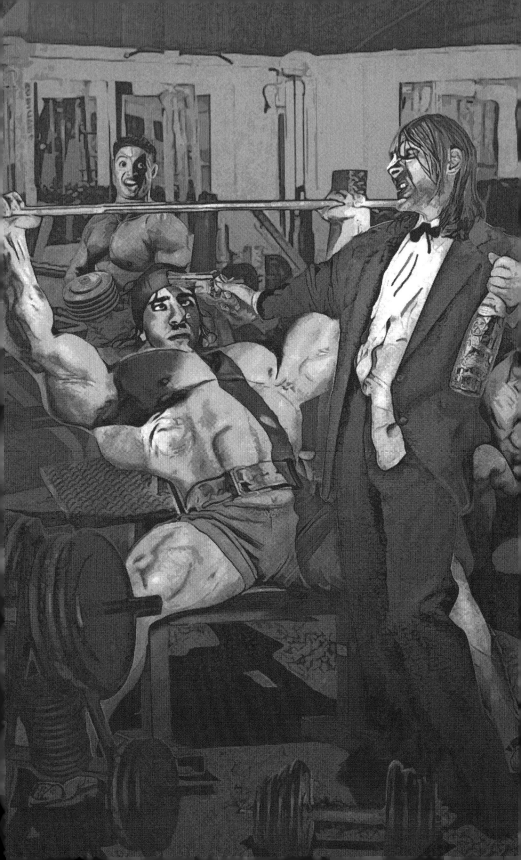

starvation—looking hungrily towards muscle matter and bone. Riding *The Binge* …

In the gym, no one moves. No one speaks.

At least a dozen muscle-junkies, each larger than the last, each in his own mid-lift, mid-press, mid-squat, stand around and stare. Eyes wide, open-mouthed, agape.

Muscleheads in thick leather lifting belts, fingerless lifting gloves and spandex shorts wait to see what will happen next.

'*What WILL happen next?*' Hiram thinks. His brain is sweating, exhausted from the heavy-lifting of the electric acid fingerprint, the opium and pink powder, the absinthe and alcohol and psychedelic frog excretions …

Musclebound brains strain to analyze the situation, to come up with a plan, a course of action. Oversized dumbbells struggle to devise a mate to Hiram's check.

"Uh … hey!" says one guy in a lateral pull machine. Sweat-soaked headband over his dim, beady eyes.

Hiram steps forward, presses the gun to Hitler's forehead. Takes a swig from the open bottle of absinthe in his free hand.

"Um, don't …" says a powerhouse in a T-shirt that reads, *Shut up brain, or I'll stop and get a Q-Tip!*

The cruel, cold-bloodedness begins to take over, filling in the empty spaces of his soul. The spaces left by his suicided mother, his disappeared father. Creeping in from the back of his brain like it always has, just before the kill—a genetic predisposition to get the job done, to look life in the face …

To murder.

Is it possible to escape and at the same time *embrace* one's upbringing?

Hiram's lips curl into a grin. A snarl.

Bruno Hitler's muscles are quivering now. Sweat pours from

his pores, streams down his face. Puddles on the floor beneath the workbench. He can barely hold up the weight any longer. Veins and tendons bulge on his arms. Teeth clenched, but he is frozen. Hiram looms over him. Holds the gun to his head.

Another fitness freak emerges from the steam room. A tiny white towel wrapped around bulging thighs. Thick white steam billowing out behind him. He stops short when he sees Hiram. Drops the towel, revealing a tiny button of a penis, shriveled by steroids and fear.

Adolf Hitler never allowed anyone to see him naked or bathing. True fact.

"I have the duty to be a fighter for truth and justice," Hiram announces flatly, unsure who he is trying to convince. "Hitler said that. He also said, 'A man can only grow strong through constant struggle.' Kudos to you, my good body sculptors! Kudos to you all and to all your hard work. But alas, the days of individual happiness have passed."

Hiram pulls the trigger. Weights crash to the floor.

And the gym is filled with the high-pitched shrieks and screams of frantic, fleeing bodybuilders.

"**T**hat bitch!"

Hitler is fuming ... "That Jew bitch took everything ... EVERYTHING! It's enough to make me want to ... make me want to ... kill 'em ALL! Every last goddamn one of 'em!!"

"You want to kill all ... the Jews?" Hiram wonders aloud.

"Fuck no!" Hitler's fingers play at the rope around his throat. "All the *women*! All the money-sucking, lying, cheating, DECEIVING women!"

Smelly and disheveled as he was—and tripping wildly, his eyes rolling in his head—Hiram had still (albeit barely) managed to talk his way past the office receptionist.

"Ma'am, I am Mr. Hiram Grange, auditor for the International Consortium of Universities. My supervisor has sent me to here to look into possible fraud, waste, and abuse allegations related to a local university that has received a sizable research grant. Is Mister Walter, er ... Hitler in?"

The psychedelic fingerprint etched into his vision like neon, he'd made his way past the receptionist. Down a corridor banked with countless cubicles (office workers furiously typing their lives away) and to a closed office door marked,

WALTER H.

Glancing back over his shoulder, the bank of cubicles seemed endless, stretching like a monorail, twisting like DNA. Heads down, people focused on their work—transformed suddenly into inmates, the office to Auschwitz. The boxcar train of cubicles thunders on, a deep roaring in Hiram's brain adds to the illusion. He blinks and turns back to the door.

Without knocking, he deftly opens the door, slips inside, and shuts it behind him. The air is stuffy. The office reeks of sweaty fear, moldy paper.

Gun drawn, ready to shoot and run, he takes aim. And stops.

Hitler is standing on his desk. Tiptoes.

The noose around his neck is strung through the central air vent.

"She took everything …" he tells Hiram. Tears in his eyes, anger in his grinding teeth.

Stacks of papers are piled on the desk, some falling to the floor where Hitler had kicked them in his suicidal ascent.

"Demoralize the enemy from within by surprise, terror, sabotage, assassination. This is the war of the future." Hitler is blubbering. "My wife said that."

"Hitler said it first," Hiram can read words like *Alimony*, *Child Support*, *Divorce* on the stacked and scattered papers.

"See, I don't want to die," Hitler is crying. Fists clenching and unclenching. "But the thing is … I feel I've lost control of the situation."

'*TELL me about it!*' Hiram thinks, slipping the *Webley* back into his pocket.

"But sometimes, we don't have a choice, do we?" Hiram's voice takes on a gentle, soothing tone. "Sometimes there really is only one solution. Sometimes, the easy way out really is the best way out …"

Hitler's eyes are pleading. He looks at Hiram, silently begging for encouragement. Approval.

"By all accounts, the experience can even be … pleasurable," Hiram continues. "Erotic. You know, Adolf Hitler himself pioneered the 'art' of autoerotic asphyxiation. After execution, he noticed that the hanged men, without exception, all had erections that lasted for hours. Some even ejaculated minutes after death …" Hiram is smiling. "True fact."

Hitler is nodding now. His toes creeping towards the edge of the desk.

"I'll leave you to yourself," Hiram backs toward the door. "Remember," he turns to Hitler, "There's a light at the end of the tunnel."

Hiram exits the office and closes the door with a soft click.

Ear pressed to the door, Hiram waits.

After a moment, a deep mournful sigh.

Then a quick scrape of heel on the lip of the desk. The taut snap of rope going tight and the POP! of vertebrae separating from vertebrae.

The iPhone chirps in Hiram's pocket. The text from Mrs. Bothwell—from *Gashleycrumb*—is urgent:

> We're running out of time, Hiram.
> Hitler's spawn CANNOT be
> allowed to survive. Hurry …
>
> —G

Staring at the words dancing on the screen, Bothwell's urgency is contagious. Still, something is amiss … If only the clouds would leave his brain …

'My kingdom for just a moment of clarity …! Something about this seems off,' thinks Hiram. Then, *'Ah, it's probably nothing …'*

Probably just the drugs.

The Binge.

But … even nothing is something. And a lot of nothing is a lot of something …

Blasting his way through the domino procession of Hitlers. First fast and wild, then slow and dirty. A murder spree to end all murder sprees. A mini Hitler holocaust …

He feels again as if he's being watched. Small hairs rising along his neck, cold fingers creeping up his spine.

Hiram spares only a moment to take a long toke of heaven's herb. And then he is off.

The Hitler freak circus awaits.

Interlude

T'he beast is larger now, but still just a loose, green, gelatinous conglomeration of three primary parts: lidless bloodshot eye, long cankerous wagging tongue, and knobby, prodding member.

Eye pressed firmly to the rip in Reality, *La Fée Verte* is laughing.

Five Hitlers down, and six to go. All according to plan.

In our world, Hiram is hunting and murdering. Killing quickly, without guilt or remorse. Without second-thought. Without care.

All according to plan …

Glimpsing to the future, that shining figure in white is nowhere to be found. His throne atop his mighty twin towers is no more—his towers themselves: nothing more than broken rubble in a broken city.

Hiram the noble, Hiram the proud. A paladin of a man, selfless philanthropist … Altruistic avenger, holy warrior … Hiram the Redeemed … Savior and saint …

'Yeah,' *La Fée Verte* cackles wildly and lets loose a long Bronx Cheer. '*THAT ain't gonna happen!*'

Like a high C shatters fine crystal, the plan is in motion to shatter Hiram's mind. Break his soul. The perfect harmonic convergence of drugs, genocide, childhood trauma, and unrepentant murder. The demon laughs. '*All set in motion the moment I donkey-punched baby Hitler in the test tube … I love it when a plan comes together!*'

Lost in reverie, *La Fée Verte* eagerly imagines the *new* future: Countless bedroom closets, concealing portals behind hangers of coats and shirts and gowns … The back walls, fleshy protrusions from the netherworld: swollen, pregnant bellies laced with sweaty-soft, downy, bristling female hairs and woodgrain … knothole navels loaded and waiting to give bloody birth, exploding green one-eyed monsters and poison afterbirth into our world, into countless closets of otherwise quiet suburban homes across middle America …

Heralding the onset of the Cascade …

But for now there is still much work to be done. The corruption of Hiram Grange will continue. Time for another e-mail from Hell.

The beast turns and pulls the hole in Reality, moving and twisting it to another perspective: A woman sleeping in a bed. The monster grins, then pokes its long waggling tongue through the hole.

The woman is older, hair in curlers, horn-rimmed glasses rest on her night table beside a glass of water. Her long nightgown, comfortable but unflattering.

The demon's tongue extends into our world, reaching, ever reaching. It brushes the woman's naked ankle, lifting the nightgown slowly up to her calf, her knee, her thigh …

But enough fooling around, *La Fée Verte* muses. No time for tricks, silly rabbit! The creature shifts its tongue ever upward. Licking over flat night-gowned stomach, over sagging braless breasts. Over nape of neck, over lightly snoring lips. Gliding gently over eyelash and ear, then to the temple. Softly caressing the temple, the monster whispers sweet nothings, stroking the subconscious, feeding the dream-state, offering dark and subversive ideas …

Food for thought …

The woman's eyes flick open, but remain glazed, asleep.

She sits up.

Walks over to her desk. Opens her e-mail and begins typing.

Digital Somnambulism. Like sleepwalking, the act of writing and sending e-mails while asleep. A true 21st Century psychosis …

She types urgently, fingers dancing over her keyboard. Without her glasses, she cannot see what she writes, but it does not matter.

Finished, she signs her e-mail: —*Gashleycrumb*

Hits SEND and climbs back into bed.

Mrs. Bothwell drifts off into forgetful sleep.

BLAM!

The crowd scatters.

Hiram is sprinting after Hitler. "*How does it feel?*" he is screaming. "*How does it FEEL?!*" The drugs have addled his brain. The acid fingerprint runs deep, labyrinthine grooves in his mind. Detours his thoughts down dark dead-ends and maze-like arroyos.

Gun drawn, Hiram is blabbering like a fool. Firing wildly, not making any sense.

"Outta my way! Who here eviscerated a god today? Hmm? Who among you good folks knows how many lives it takes to skin Schrödinger's Cat? *Out of my way, I say!*"

BLAM!

People are screaming, babies crying, brakes are screeching.

Dogs are barking.

"*Bolivia exports tin!*" hollers Hiram.

BLAM!

The bullet ricochets off the sidewalk. A pedestrian—an elderly woman in a fur coat with a *Saks Fifth Ave.* bag clutched in her painted claws—screams as sharp shrapnel shards of sidewalk pepper her overly makeuped face, leaving a dotwork pattern of blood.

BLAM!

There's a *Yelp!* and one of the dogs is down.

Hitler doesn't stop.

"*It is what it is!*" cries Hiram.

The street is crowded with the Upper West Side lunch crowd. Shoppers and diners and businessmen, all crowding the streets and filling the sidewalk bistro tables. New York's elite gawk in outrage. Scramble and dive for cover.

Hitler is breathing heavy. Running for dear life. Full sprint. Legs pumping, fist clutching a handful of leashes. A dozen dogs in his charge, one down, eleven panting and drooling, enjoying the unexpected run.

Hiram gives chase. *"Hot as HELL on Sunday ...!"* he bellows, reloading his gun.

Hitler is dressed in knee-length knickers and a white, short-sleeve, button-down-collar shirt. Leading the race is a collection of ugly little dogs—poodles and Shi Tzus. Rich people's dogs.

Eli Hitler, professional dog walker.

New York's Upper West side is all abustle with panic. Horns blare. The streetlights and neon crosswalk signs are psychedelically blinding. Not far off a siren begins to wail.

Heat hangs in the air. The sun beats down. The exotic smells of Middle Eastern street vendor food fills the air, mixing with the stench of baking, uncollected garbage in the street, steam and urine rising from the subway grates.

The dead dog drags behind. Bouncing and scraping along the sidewalk. A thick trail of blood and fur. Leash taut.

BLAM! BLAM!

Another dog down.

"Don't look now but Sadie's dilated at eight centimeters ..." shrieks Hiram. *"Breathe through the contractions, baby—we're having a BABY! A beautiful blue-eyed boy! Boo-yaah!"*

Another shot and a third dog drops. Hitler begins to slow, the canine anchors dragging him down.

Hiram feels a dull ache in his left knee—a throbbing reminder of an injury he'd received four years earlier, while chasing apparitions through the piss-stinking alleys of Halifax. "*Some whitefish for the man who hasn't eaten in millennia?*" the stoned killer inquires, all crazy eyes and flailing arms. Overturning a bistro table—dishes shatter and terrified diners seek cover. "*Caviar!*" screams Hiram, never breaking stride.

BLAM!

The bullet goes wild, taking down an innocent. A young man in a suit. He crumples to his knees, dying in a pool of his own blood. Choking and gurgling into his cellular headset.

'*Damn, innocents!*' thinks Hiram. And then, 'Innocents *or* inner sense? *There ARE no innocents in this world …*'

BLAM!

"*Not a man!*" Hiram's nonsensical rant takes on an edge of hysteria. "*We're giving birth to lizards and weasels!*" Tears fill eyes so dilated there's no discernible iris. "*I wanna see my baby—I wanna hold my son …!*"

BLAM! Another dead-weight doggie, slowing Hitler down. Trailing blood on the sidewalk. *CLICK.*

The empty shell.

(His mother's suicide shell)

Hiram's deft fingers quickly reload, his sprinting legs never breaking pace. Hot empty shells fall to the ground, bouncing off the pavement.

(But not his mother's shell, never his mother's shell)

Hiram is breathing heavy now. Elbowing and pistol-whipping his way through the posh, overdressed crowd.

No matter how hot it was, Adolf Hitler would never remove his coat in public. True fact.

BLAM! BLAM! BLAM!

Three shots, three dogs.

The leash handles are a tangled knot around Hitler's wrist. He's unable to release the dead dogweight.

Pulled from both sides—barking, running dogs ahead, dead, bloody dogs behind—Hitler stops. Turns to Hiram, his eyes pleading.

"WAIT! STOP! You don't have to! The Green Dude ... He told me—"

BLAM!

Right between the eyes. Hitler goes down. Tangled in a mess of leashes, yelping dogs and blood.

People stare from the windows of gridlocked cars. The dogs that are still alive are sniffing, nuzzling their dead walker. Lapping up the expanding pool of blood.

Hiram steps forward, gun hot and smoking. Eyes bloodshot, dark rings beneath them. A dirty scruff of beard, face stained with blood and grime.

"*Not a man!*" he cries madly.

The crowd parts.

Hiram staggers up to the bar, but Sadie is nowhere in sight.

His head is still reeling, but his thoughts are coming clearer now. Less fragmented. The thumbprint is a swirling vortex in his brain, sucking stray thoughts down its rusty drain, and gurgling up mucky ideas. Mucky ideas like the strange flowers for Sadie ...

UberNacht is hopping. Bar patrons to either side back away from Hiram, holding their noses. Hiram raps on the polished oak of the bar with bare, bloody knuckles and winks. Trixie, a young bartendress in ripped fishnets, black nail polish, and a face full of piercings, winks back.

"Hiram!" she cries, "Ooh flowers! For me?" she bats her eyes.

"Just kidding," she hands him a nearly full bottle of *Bombay Sapphire*. "Sadie's around here somewhere ... maybe on break ..."

Hiram nods and heads for the back of the room.

Flowers clenched in a fist behind his back, the writhing, pressing throng of dancers and drinkers hurriedly part to make way for Hiram. Gagging and retching, backing away, holding noses.

Down the stairs, into the unused supply room.

Sadie and Edsel are sitting cross-legged in the corner. Spellbound in deep conversation, they don't even notice Hiram. Edsel is still handcuffed to the shelves, pink fuzz and Dago balls now matted with sweat and grime.

"I don't *feel* like Hitler ..." Edsel is saying.

"Yeah. Well, you sure LOOK like him," Sadie replies.

Hitler wrinkles his nose. "What is that *smell?*"

Hiram thrusts the flowers forward as they turn to him. Hitler swallows hard. Eyes watering, he pinches his nose with his free hand. Sadie jumps up and rushes into Hiram's arms.

"Hiram, really? A Corpse flower?"

Amorphophallus titanum, the deep purple, phallic-shaped stem is surrounded by blood-red petals. The stamen emits a noxious, overpowering odor of rotten meat.

Hiram smiles.

"I love it!" Sadie takes the flower, presses her nose to it and inhales deeply. "It's sooo ... you!"

"That's disgusting," Hitler is gagging in the corner.

"Oh, you shut up," Sadie's goth, shadowed eyes are fixed on Hiram. Black lipstick curls into a smile. Wordlessly she rubs her tummy and her smile widens. On tiptoes, pulling his ear down to her lips. "I'm gonna find a vase to put this in ..." She pecks his cheek and exits the door. "Sooo cool ..." she's mumbling.

Hiram turns to Hitler. "Where's the next one?" he demands.

"She's something else," Hitler sighs. Eyes lingering on the open door. Already, the smell of death is leaving the room. "I hope you know how much she—"

"I know!" Hiram barks. Grabs Hitler by the scruff of his neck. Squeezes. "Where do I find your next brother?"

"*Do you, now?*" Hitler ignores the demand. Locks his eyes on Hiram's. His voice drips venom "*Do you? Do you know her? Do you know how she was emancipated at sixteen? You know about the abuse? How her father used to rape her? How he stepped in front of a commuter rail the day the court granted her emancipation? How her mother overdosed on diet pills? Six weeks in a coma before she finally kicked it? You think you know her, huh?*"

Hiram is dumbfounded. Some of this he knew, but not all. How this shitty little Hitler knock-off could get off thinking—

"No wonder she's so obsessed with death," Edsel continues. "She's eighteen, and she needs someone to talk to. She needs a friend," Hitler takes a deep breath, braces himself and continues. "What she *doesn't* need is some opium-smoking lunatic artificially doing the nasty *in vitro* with his rotten seed ... Believe me, I know how that story ends. Do you really think she's ready to have a—"

Hiram explodes.

Slams Hitler against the dusty shelves. Bottles topple and shatter on the floor all around them. An ancient bag of flour and rat droppings tears open, filling the room with its dust and painting them a ghostly white.

"*Who the fuck do you think you are?*" Hiram roars.

Hitler's head is bobbling from side to side as Hiram shakes him. "Her friend," he stammers. "Not some monster just pretending to be. I know what you are—"

Hiram grins. "There's only one thing you need to know about me." He cracks his knuckles. "And that is that I am going to make you tell me where the rest of your wretched clone-brothers are."

Hitler is crying now. "I love her …" he sobs.

"No you don't," says Hiram.

"You promised you would kill me."

"No worries," Hiram whispers darkly. "I keep my promises. But first things first …"

Eighth little Hitler, the only one who blogs.

"**W**ho are you and how did you get in here?" Gabe Hitler demands.

"I'm the locksmith … and I'm the locksmith." Hiram chuckles to himself, calling forth the old line.

"Close the door," Hitler orders. "Lock it. Wanna drink?" he offers Hiram the half-empty bottle of *Mezcal* in his hand.

Hiram slides the lock and takes the bottle. Long swig, his eyes focused on the worm, dead and pickled floating at the bottom. His fingers caress the *Webley*.

Hiram takes a second long pull of tequila.

"What's going on here?" The small room is practically bare. Just a wobbly card table with two laptop computers balanced precariously on it. A desktop computer on the floor beneath. Stacks of old pizza boxes and empty beer bottles. And a thin cot. Hiram squints at the computers. Swastika screensavers bounce lazily about the screens. "What're you up to?"

A toilet flushes and a door opens on the other side of the room. A man in his forties. Wearing faded jeans, ripped at the knees, and Birkenstocks. A loose tan T-shirt, and impossibly long brown hair reaching to the buckle of his belt. He smiles warmly.

"That's Jesus," Hitler introduces the man. "And you are …?"

Hiram's eyes dart between the two, fingers stroking his gun. "Sirs, I am Mr. Hiram Grange of the OIRA … Did you say … Jesus?"

Both men nod.

"One of three," Hitler grins. Hiram holds out the tequila, but Jesus waves it away.

"One of … My god, man! Is he a *clone?*" Hiram is astonished.

Both men laugh. Jesus shakes his head.

"Not a clone," Hitler smiles. "Maybe you should sit down, though." He slides a stool from the card table to Hiram. Hiram sits. "This is some heavy shit …"

"You ever heard of the Three Christs of Ypsilanti?" Hitler asks.

"There's really only just the one," Jesus interrupts. "Me." He indicates himself, poking his thumb to his chest.

"*Riiiight* … anyway," Hitler continues, but is interrupted again, this time by a knocking at the door. Hiram jumps.

"Why don't you go take care of that," Hitler turns to Jesus.

Jesus shrugs and walks to the door. Opens it a crack and peeks through, then steps out into the apartment hallway and closes it behind him.

"Who is it?" Hiram glances nervously at the door.

"No one, man," Hitler grins. "Probably just Einstein."

Hiram opens his mouth to speak, but Hitler cuts him off. "Just kidding, man. We ordered a pizza."

"Jesus?"

"He'll be out there for a few minutes," Hitler says. "He doesn't like it when I talk about Ypsilanti. Makes him anxious."

"What's Ypsilanti?"

"Not what. Where. It's a town near Ann Arbor, Michigan. They had a nuthouse there … you know, an institution, an asylum … And back in the fifties, they did an experiment."

Hiram's head is swimming. He can hear Jesus outside bartering with the pizza delivery man.

"At one point they had three residents—inmates, *patients*—each of whom believed himself to be Christ incarnate. And instead of trying to actually help these people, what do you think those good doctors did?"

Hiram shakes his head.

"They put them all together to live in the same dorm room for a year."

"Why?"

" … " Hitler scratches his chin. "Well … why not? To see what would happen, I guess …"

"What happened?" Hiram is intrigued.

"Nothing, really. After a year together, each of them came out of the experiment more convinced than ever that he was really Jesus, and that the other two were filthy, lying imposters."

"Doesn't sound like much of an experiment."

"No, I suppose it doesn't. But that's not all … Like I said, this was back in the fifties."

Hiram pokes his thumb towards the door. "That Jesus out there doesn't look a day older than forty …"

"That's what I'm *saying* …!" Hitler is nodding. "Like I said, man. He claims to be the real deal."

"That's impossible," Hiram frowns. The *Webley* a heavy lump in his pocket.

"That's what I thought, but I checked it out. He was at Ypsilanti. His fingerprints match. So does his birthmark."

Before Hiram can reply, the door swings open and Jesus wanders in with the pizza. Hitler rushes over to the door. Slams it and bolts it, then turns to his friend.

"Did you tip him?" Hitler asks.

Jesus nods.

"You sure?"

"Yes," Jesus insists. Averts his eyes. Stares at the floor.

Hitler frowns, but lets it go.

"It's the reincarnation of Paul Revere's horse, man … and we'd all better be nervous!" Jesus is munching on a slice of pizza with anchovies and green peppers.

Hiram is suddenly hungrier than he's ever been. He grabs a slice and takes a bite. Chews. Tries to swallow, but *The Binge* won't let him.

His stomach turns and flips. Dangerous nausea, deep aches and sharp pain in his kidneys, his liver. He drops the slice on the floor and reaches for the *Mezcal*.

"Adolf ordered his staff to secretly film the torture and execution of political prisoners, for his own personal collection. He had a huge collection of pornographic pictures." Hiram swigs the *Mezcal*. "True fact."

Gabe Hitler counters. "Dude *loved* the circus. Got off on the idea that the performers were risking their lives just to please him."

"He was a vegetarian," adds Jesus.

Hiram takes another swig of Mezcal. The bottle is almost empty.

"He had impeccable handwriting," Hitler says. "When Carl Jung saw a sample of it in 1937, he remarked: '*Behind this handwriting I recognize the typical characteristics of a man with essentially feminine instinct.*'"

Jesus chimes in. "He was a chronic pacer. He would always pace inside rooms, always whistling the same tune, and always walking diagonally across the room, from corner to corner."

"Come on," says Gabe. "How do *you* know that? Were you there?"

"Maybe I was," Jesus frowns. "Anyway, show him ..." Jesus nods towards the computers on the desk.

"Show me what, Jesus?" Hiram asks.

"Call me Leon," Jesus insists. "Our blogsite, that's what."

"Conspiracies," adds Hitler, waking a laptop from its sleep. "The truth, the whole truth, and nothing but the truth ..."

Hiram suddenly remembers the pill—*The Big H*—nestled in his pocket. *The trooth, da whole trooth, and nuttin' but da TROOTH!* Livingstone Hitler had called it ...

"JFK, UFOs ... Bigfoot. Stuff like that," Jesus nods offhandedly.

"Dead babies beneath ground zero," Hitler adds. "The twelve of us clawed our way out, but you don't think for a second that we were the first attempt, do you? The only ones? How many hundreds, thousands ... hundreds of thousands of aborted clones do you think came before us?"

"A virtual Hitler Holocaust ..." adds Jesus.

"Not to mention all the failed attempts. The ones they made 'disappear' ... Don't get me started on the bus load of Hitlers they drove off the cliff in Wyoming."

"Where are your brothers now?" Hiram's fingers tighten around the grip of the *Webley*. "Have you seen any of them?" Hiram swallows the last gulp of tequila, wincing as it burns his tongue. The worm slides down his throat.

"If you tell a big enough lie ..." Jesus is saying, "tell it frequently enough, people will believe it." He indicates the computer. The blog. "You'll even begin to believe it yourself."

"Make the lie big, make it simple, keep on saying it, and eventually they'll believe it," Hitler adds.

"We're shining a light THROUGH all the lies." Jesus smiles proudly. "Our blog is a lighthouse to an island of truth."

Hitler taps a key. On the screen:

JESUS AND HITLER WALK INTO A BAR ...

Bartender: What is this, a joke!?

Welcome to THE TRUTH: A Blog

"There's something in the air, man ... something's going on right beneath our noses, right beneath our brains ..." Jesus is shaking his head. "Can't you feel it?"

Hitler takes up the train of thought. "All this stuff about love your brother, nature versus nurture, love versus mating instinct, sexual attraction, desire, genetic predisposition … It all looks good on paper—"

"But no one really believes it in a conscious, day-to-day reality sort've way," Jesus finishes. Smiles his gentle smile. "In our blog, we're setting things right. Pulling the plug. Popping the bubble."

"Telling it like it is," Hitler says. Then, "Hey! What're you doing?"

Hiram is holding the *Webley* on Hitler. Point blank, finger on trigger.

"The truth dies here," says Hiram. "Sorry, chum."

Suddenly, an animal growl.

Fast as lightning, Jesus is on him. Biting, clawing, gouging at his eyes, pulling his hair. A knee in the groin, and Hiram's testicles are slammed, smashed against his body. Pain explodes in his belly. He drops the gun. Staggers to the floor, Jesus on top of him. With sudden horror, Hiram realizes that he's in for the fight of his life …

Desperately grabbing the empty bottle of *Mezcal*, Hiram brings it up hard. Glass shatters, slicing Jesus from temple to chops. A loose flap of skin hangs from his lips. The Christ bares his teeth, grins a bloody grin, and reaches for Hiram's throat.

Waiting until the last possible moment before rolling quickly to the left, Hiram avoids Jesus' powerful lunge. Hiram darts out his foot and sweeps Hitler's leg, taking him solidly down. Gabe lands heavily on the floor, coccyx cracking with a sharp report.

Hiram is on his feet. He grabs the bulky desktop computer, holding it between him and Jesus. Keeping the Ypsilanti savior at bay, like a tamer to a lion.

"You bastard!" screams Jesus, wiping blood from his split face into his eyes, his hair, his teeth. "I'll kill you, you motherfucker!" he roars.

Groaning on the floor, Hitler is reaching for the *Webley*. Keeping Jesus in his sights, Hiram deftly maneuvers around and kicks it away across the floor.

Jesus lunges.

Hiram grabs the monitor, brings it sharply up. Catches Jesus on the chin. The screen shatters in a shower of glass and electricity, jolting Jesus backwards into the table.

Hiram pulls the *Pritchard* bayonet from its concealed sheath at the small of his back. Jesus has retrieved the jagged neck of the *Mezcal* bottle. The two square off.

Hitler is trying to crawl away, but Hiram brings his boot down hard, shattering Gabe's knee. Jesus is laughing now. Blood is dripping from his chin.

He thrusts the broken bottle forward, catching Hiram's upper arm. Coat, shirt and skin are shredded. Hiram's sleeve fills with blood. It drips from his fingers. Jesus has hit an artery.

Hitler is clawing his way towards the door.

With an animal shriek, Jesus launches himself at Hiram. Strong fingers wrap around Hiram's neck. Uncut nails dig into the back of his skull. Hiram can't breathe.

The room is growing dark, the psychedelic fingerprint glows brightly. Beckoning. Blood pounds in Hiram's ears.

Jesus lifts him by the neck and slowly walks him across the room.

Hiram's dangling toes are scraping the floor. His arms are limp.

Jesus is laughing maniacally. Heading for the window.

Twelve stories up.

His foot lands on the *Webley* and slips.

They go down hard. Hiram a rag doll on top of Jesus.

Blood is everywhere, and when Hiram's sight returns he can see the hilt of his knife jutting from Jesus' side.

Hiram has to twist it to pull it out, but no matter: The man is dead.

Hitler is still alive, but not for long.

Wiping Jesus' blood on his pants, Hiram stands up. Retrieves the *Webley* with his good arm.

Takes aim.

BLAM!

Another Hitler down. And a Jesus, to boot.

On one of the laptop computers, Hitler's blog reads:

**What good fortune for governments
that the people do not think.**

Don't it feel like the wind is always howlin'?
Don't it seem like there's never any light!
Once a day, don't you wanna throw the towel in?
It's easier than puttin' up a fight . . .

Hiram is seated in the third row, tending his wounds and popping magic mushrooms—strange lichen and exotic pills stolen from Livingstone Hitler's lab. The fight with Jesus still fresh in his mind.

His arm in a tourniquet. Eighteen stitches with thread pulled from his father's coat. The bleeding has slowed to a clotting ooze.

No one's there when your dreams at night get creepy!
No one cares if you grow . . . or if you shrink!
No one dries when your eyes get wet an' weepy . . .

Hiram is surrounded by men. The theater is nearly empty, but maybe a dozen burly guys have come out to see the all-male West Village production of *Little Orphan Annie*.

All eyes are fixed on the stage.

No one even spares Hiram a glance.

It's the hard-knock life! For us!
Got no folks to speak of, so,
It's the hard-knock row we hoe!

Hiram was born with a shrewd intellect. He'd spent his life developing and nurturing an encyclopedic knowledge of the darker parts of the world—from the white sex-slavery cartels of Bolivia to the occult wizards of Siberia. But nothing in his experience could have prepared him for Little Orphan Annie . . .

Little Orphan Annie isn't so little.

Though, Hiram supposes, the actor portraying her is just as much an orphan as she is. More so.

Red yarn Raggedy Ann hair and oversized, finger-painted freckles are in stark contrast to the dark, one-third Hitler mustache on Annie's upper lip. The other orphans, twinks every one, are waifish and petite—the tallest only comes up to Hitler's shoulders.

> *When I'm stuck in a day,*
> *That's gray,*
> *And lonely,*
> *I just stick out my chin,*
> *And grin,*
> *And say,*
> *Oh …*

Hiram's ticket had been waiting at Will-Call, arranged by the elusive Mrs. Bothwell. Under the codename *Gashleycrumb*.

At the mere thought of her name, Hiram's iPhone chirps. Another message. Marked HIGH PRIORITY.

> *How many Hitlers to go?*
> *Time is of the essence …*
> *—Gashleycrumb*

Hiram furiously types back,

> *Fuck off. Almost done.*
> *After this I'm taking a sabbatical.*
> *—HG*

Stuffs the phone in his pocket. Checks the *Webley*. Five rounds, one empty shell. Pops another pill. A strange, unidentified pill.

While Hitler is singing, nails on glass, Hiram removes *The Big H* from his pocket. The final solution. Hitler's party pill. The end-all, be-all.

Sniffs it. Nothing.

Licks it. Nothing, just sugarcoated ink casing.

When? he asks the thing.

Soon, it tells him.

> *The sun'll come out ... Tomorrow ...*
> *Bet your bottom dollar that tomorrow ...*
> *There'll be sun!*

Hiram stands up. Makes for the bathroom, but slips into the wings. Over the red velvet rope and backstage.

He's waiting in Hitler's makeup room as the first act finale is building. Muffled and heavy with bass, he can still hear Lil' Hitler singing his heart out.

> *Just thinkin' about tomorrow,*
> *Clears away the cobwebs,*
> *And the sorrow ...*

The crowd roars its applause.

Moments later, Hitler enters his makeup room, a sweaty, disheveled mess. Eyeliner running, dark, wet rings under his armpits. He spies Hiram.

"Darling, you shouldn't be back here ..." he takes a grease pen from his mirrored table. "Come on ... gimme, gimme ..."

"Give you what?" Hiram is genuinely surprised. Hitler hasn't noticed the gun resting in Hiram's lap.

Hitler sighs dramatically. "What. Ev. Er. Something to WRITE on ... Hurry up, hurry up ... You DO want my autograph, don't you?" Hitler takes on a sly look, "Or you come back here for something else, honey?"

"I don't think so," Hiram is more confused than anything else.

"Fine." Hitler shows him the hand. "Starts with *double-you* ... ends in *hat*. Continues on with *ever* ..."

"Um," says Hiram.

"In other words, sugar ..." Hitler bats his eyes. "Get out. I'm back on in ten, and I've got to gargle or my voice'll never be ready for the poison of the crowd. Out now ... Shoo ... shoo ..."

Hiram doesn't move. "What's with the mustache?" he asks. Digging at Hitler, prompting him to anger. Testing his mettle.

"Don't you worry about my mustache, Sweetie. If it's not the fashion now, it will be soon enough," Hitler winks. Adjusts his orange locks. "Besides, only when I'm disguised am I really myself."

"Are you Jamaican?" Hiram asks.

"Huh?"

"I asked you if you were Jamaican, sir," Hiram repeats his question.

"Jamaican?"

"Yes. Are you Jamaican?"

"No ..." Hitler is flummoxed. "Why do you ask?"

"Because you're Ja-makin' me crazy ...!" Hiram pulls the trigger.

BLAM!

Runs for the door. But backstage the exit is blocked.

Actors and VIPs mill around, smoking by the open fire exit. Hiram considers rushing through them, but it seems too risky. Too many civilians. Enough to describe his face, point the direction of his escape ...

Hiram ducks back into the dressing room. Removes Hitler's wig. Picks up a tube of makeup.

Shuffling across the stage, in front of the curtain, Hiram meets thunderous applause.

Dressed in Hitler's orange Annie locks, clown lipstick smearing his face, dark eyeliner blackening his eyes—Hiram does the one-step, two-step across the stage.

Standing ovation.

The mushrooms are kicking in, big time.

Whistles and catcalls.

Exit stage right.

Escape into darkness.

Edsel Hitler is still handcuffed to the shelves. Sadie's iPod is in his hand, the headphone earbuds in his ears. He is lost in a world of his own.

Hiram is hovering over him before the little Hitler even looks up. Just stares at Hiram coldly. Doesn't say a word.

('*Be nicer to him …*' Sadie had implored. 'I *want you to be nice … My nice, nice man …*')

But Sadie isn't here.

Hiram tears the buds from Hitler's ears. "What are you listening to?"

Hitler nods at the earbuds. "Go ahead."

"Hmph." Hiram places them in his own ears. Expecting the worst—*Mein Kampf* translated and read aloud by William Shatner; or that techno-industrial noise that Sadie and the *UberNacht* crowd seemed to thrive upon … but nothing could have prepared Hiram for the pure, orchestral beauty that fills his ears. Poetry in motion. Philosophy and strings. Pure, unadulterated love and the voice of an angel. Shadows of Bach's *Toccata and Fugue*, but punctuated with a hip, modern sentimentality.

All at once he is overwhelmed by a music so powerful, so soulful, so *intense* that he feels he might lose himself in its beauty.

> *Another day, another dollar, another war, another tower,*
> *So we pray to as many different Gods as there are flowers …*

Unable to help himself, Hiram's eyes are welling with tears. His throat locked in a sob. The psychedelic neon fingerprint in his mind expands and glows and dances. The moment is transcendental. The fingerprint in his brain bounces and throbs in time with the beat.

Glows with the melody. The lyrics seem handcrafted for him—speak to him, in him and through him—

Who will save your soul, after all the lies that you told?
Who will save your soul if you won't save your own?

'*Who* will *save my soul?*' thinks Hiram. '*Who* can?'

He slumps against the wall. Slides to the floor. The tears are flowing freely now.

Hitler watches, expressionless.

Hiram closes his eyes …

… And wakes in a puddle of vomit.

'*There's blood in my vomit,*' he thinks. '*Or is there vomit in my blood?*'

Sadie is standing over him. "What HAPPENED to you?" she demands. "You're a mess …" She's dabbing at his scraped chin with a wet napkin. Tight, clean bandages on his freshly wrapped arm. "When's the last time you've eaten?"

Hiram laughs. It's a mean, horrible, self-deprecating laugh. '*Eaten?*' he thinks, '*The damned don't eat …*'

Sadie places her palms on his cold, pale cheeks. Tears of dark eyeliner streak down his cheeks. His clownish *Orphan Annie* lipstick is smudged. "Hiram, are you okay?"

"No, Sadie. Not even close to okay," his throat is parched and dry. Dirty curls of an impossibly red hue fall over his forehead into his eyes. The Annie wig is lopsided, backwards. It hurts to speak. "Who will save my soul, Sadie?" he croaks. "Who can possibly save my soul?"

"Save your …? Hiram, what's happened? What's going on?"

"Same old, same old," his voice little more than a dry whisper. "Never you mind, my sweet, sexy Sadie." He laughs bitterly. "This old soul can't be saved, anyway. Doesn't deserve to be."

"Hiram …" she grips him by the shoulders. "How could you say that? What sort of father could ever think such a thing?"

He looks at her darkly, through pitch-black over-expanded pupils. There's no reasoning with eyes like that.

He turns away from her. "Who's gonna forgive the things I've done?" he asks the wall. "The things I'm still going to do …"

"I don't know, Hiram … I don't know what you're talking about. I don't know what you've done, and I don't want … But who will *forgive* you? If that's what you're asking … maybe no one … Maybe me …" She tries to turn him to face her, but his lanky frame is firm, immovable.

"But that's not what matters, Hiram. What matters is that you forgive yourself."

Hiram laughs. Pulls away from Sadie.

Stands up and heads for the door.

"You always have the power to forgive yourself," Sadie calls after him.

But if he hears her, he shows no sign.

"**A**nd *these signs shall follow them that believe: In my name shall they cast out devils; they shall speak with new tongues …*

"*They shall take up serpents; and if they drink any deadly thing, it shall not hurt them; they shall lay hands on the sick, and they shall recover …!*

"*That's* Mark 16:17-18, *bro …!*" Hitler stands at the altar, holding a snake in each hand. Long and writhing. As thick as Polish sausages, and full of life.

Panamint Speckled Rattlesnakes. Extremely venomous.

Rattlers rattling, teeth bared and violently hissing—the snakes are pissed.

"*Hallelujah!*" shrieks Father Danny, the only person in attendance to Ezekiel Hitler's clergy-in-training session. The dust-filled church, empty save for the two men and the snakes. Father Danny leaps up from his clapboard pew. "*Praise the Lord!*"

The red-haired reverend drops to his knees. The ramshackle church is filled with dust and unused clapboards. A chicken wire snake pen sits atop the altar.

Hiram watches. Peeking in through a break in a stained glass window.

"*Behold, I give unto you power to tread on serpents and scorpions, and over all the power of the enemy: and nothing shall by any means hurt you ...*" Hitler screams.

"Luke 10:19!" answers Father Danny at the top of his lungs. "Nice!" He falls to the ground, writhing on the floor with a snake of his own, a tremendous brown Cottonmouth. "Are you ready for tomorrow's sermon?" he yells, madder than a bucketload of snakes.

"Yes! Praise God!" answers Hitler, dropping to his own knees. "The Apocalypse isn't coming, it's here! All herald the Reckoning, the Rapture, the *Cascade* ...!"

It is always more difficult to fight against faith than against knowledge. Adolf Hitler said this. True fact.

Hiram cocks the hammer of his *Webley* and dives through the stained glass window.

Rainbow shards rain down everywhere.

Hitler shrieks.

"Heathen!" cries Father Danny. The older man is muscular, broad-shouldered. Tight, knotted muscles betray the wiry strength of the truly insane. "Foul Hell-Spawn! I condemn thee!"

Hiram lands on both feet.

Boots planted firmly on the ground. Gun blazing.

A cool Appalachian wind blows through the shattered window.

Dust billows in small tornadoes around the church—the stale room is opened to the lush outside air for the first time in decades.

Splinters of colored glass and wood fill the air as Hiram empties round after round.

Hitler is down. Down, but still alive.

Father Danny is screaming in shrill, Pentecostal fury. "*How dare you? How DARE you!* Who says that we are not under the special protection of God?"

Sprinting to the altar, the red-haired celebrant grips the snake pen and pulls … Pulls the chicken wire enclosure over and onto himself, releasing the vile serpents.

Covered in snakes, the man begins to laugh. Banded Rock Rattlesnakes and Western Diamondbacks dangle from his arms, squirm beneath his shirt.

The floor is writhing.

Dusky Pigmy Rattlesnakes glide across the floor. Florida Cottonmouths coil and rear their toothy heads.

They're fast. Hiram is surrounded.

Eastern Coral Snakes circle his feet, hissing and biting at his boots. Striking his ankles, his calves, his thighs.

Father Danny is laughing. His red hair like hellfire. He holds two fistfuls of snakes—none are biting him. He throws them at Hiram.

"*God is in the details!*" he yells with insane glee.

Teeth beyond count sink into Hiram's flesh. Venom stings to the bones. He can feel his flesh swelling. Burning. Itching. His clothes feel too tight.

He's losing consciousness.

The world is blurring around him. His heart is pounding like a jackhammer, ready to explode.

A poisonous tang fills the back of his throat, sick foam collects beneath his tongue.

His nostrils register the poisoned smells of pig shit and turpentine.

The psychedelic fingerprint turns a sickly green …

He collapses.

"*Hee hee hee …!*" Father Danny giggles. "Looks like we got a nonbeliever here …"

"Take it up with your god …" Hiram is drooling, his voice no more than a hoarse whisper.

He falls to the ground, covered in snakes. But not before firing off two final shots.

Hiram awakens to blinding fever.

There's a red tint to the world. The front of his shirt is covered in thick, black bile.

He tries to stand, but the pain is excruciating—his legs are swollen to three times their normal width. His boots look like tiny doll shoes. His pants are torn, the flesh of his legs puckered and red. Cratered with pus-filled snakebites. He's swollen like a peach.

His head is swimming.

Most, but not all, of the snakes are gone. Left for greener pastures. Or for darkened spaces between the walls and under the floor. The few that are left are spent, coiled and sleeping, paying Hiram no mind.

The most intense pain he's ever felt rips through Hiram's stomach. He leans forward and dry heaves. Tears squirt from his eyes. More black bile splashes onto the floor.

The psychedelic fingerprint burns his brain. Tells him he's dying. Tells him he'd be better off dead.

Hitler and Father Danny lie cold, pale, lifeless on the floor of the church. Each sports a tiny, black bullet hole perfectly placed between the eyes.

Gripping his sides, Hiram pushes, slides himself across the floor of the church. Over to Father Danny.

Swollen hands rifle through Danny's garments. Reaching into pockets, groping into folds. Grasping at anything—closing around two objects: one slick and hard, the other pliable and soft.

More than Hiram had any right to hope for. More than he deserved: a silver flask of *Old Kentucky* and a leather case with syringe and anti-venom. Seems Father Danny had all his bases covered. Hiram smiles—right about now, he would be taking it up with his god.

Hiram takes a long pull of whisky from the flask. Then another. And another.

Gingerly at first, then aggressively, he begins sucking venom from his wounds. Spitting it on the floor. Pouring whisky in the wounds.

He slides the hypo into the anti-venom bottle. Taps out the air with his finger, and plunges the needle into his chest.

Depressing the plunger, Hiram's body is wracked with spasms. He can't breathe.

The fingerprint expands and explodes in his brain. His eyes bulge from his head.

And then the tension begins to melt away.

Hiram sits in silence. Cold, clammy sweat drenching his blood-and-bile stained clothes. He loses track of time. Sleeps and wakes, sleeps and wakes …

And when ready, he stands.

Walks to the door …

And with poisoned eyes, he faces the bright sunlight.

Hiram is in Hell.

The junkyard is poison. Poison and rust.

Dirt and filth. A dump.

The reek of rotting food fills the air. Garbage and maggots and rats and infection abound.

Oil and decay—endless acres of abandoned cars fill every inch of the place. Piled on top of each other, as many as five tall. Not an unbroken window among them.

Washing machines and dryers, dead refrigerators, and mountains of unrecognizable metal, plastic and rust everywhere. Acres of sordid, polluted landfill.

Toxic barrels and industrial waste.

Junkyard dogs roam the narrow paths and alleys through the debris. But even these vicious dogs will not approach the bears.

As sick as he is—snake venom still coursing through his veins, held barely at bay by the anti-venom—as sick as he is, Hiram cannot tear his eyes away from the bears.

A dozen of them, at least—they've claimed their territory in the junkyard. Staked their ground. With huge paws and impossible strength, the animals dig through the rubble and debris. Bending bumpers, overturning cars—heaving and throwing tires, washers and bathtubs—it's an act unparalleled by any circus.

The snake poison is a sickly, but intriguing, new high—Hiram is spellbound by the bears' visceral, atavistic, primal show.

Hiram is fascinated. Rapt.

If he is going to die, he wants to die watching these bears.

But he knows he's not dying, however strongly it might feel like he is. His snakebitten legs turned blue, then purple ... now heading towards black. His mind is sick. Even the steady dose of psychedelics can't ward off the pain and dementia. Miserable? Yes. But dying? It had been close—closer than Hiram could ever remember cutting it. But thanks to whisky and anti-venom, he would pull through.

Like he always did.

(*The Binge*—the loop-de-loop and long, hard fall ... how much further still to go?)

His dark thoughts turn towards Sadie. Towards his unborn child. His spawn. The fruits of the womb ... What evils would his son know in his life? What strange genetic demons would he inherit? What darkness would haunt him?

What wretched traits could he (Hiram) possibly have worth passing on? That shouldn't be snuffed out at the first opportunity?

What in Hiram is worthwhile? Redeemable?

What is left of his tattered, abused soul?

The answer, he knows, is, of course ... nothing.

No one should be condemned to inherit Hiram's awful legacy. The child should not be cursed to be born.

Hiram would wish his life, his genes, on no one.

Dark thoughts and leftover poison. Hiram is immersed in the bears' acrobatics, brooding and watching them throw their junk—when he is suddenly startled from his reverie.

"Whatchoo doin' here-ah?" Hitler is wearing bib overalls and no shirt. An unlit, half-smoked cigarette dangles from his mouth. "You t'ain't s'posed ta be hear-ah!"

A wave—the strongest yet—of drunken, poison, psychedelic dementia washes over Hiram. The world ripples. There's a sick sizzling-frying-buzzing in his head.

The world tilts. Goes out of focus.

One of the bears picks up a strange object and tosses it. Hiram recognizes his father's head. Dead eyes rolling in their sockets, tossed from bear to bear ...

Is this a junkyard of the mind? A junkyard of the soul? Junkyard of dreams ... Metaphoric purgatory or actual hell? Another bear picks up a small object that glints in the sun. A glass vial, filled with a milky white liquid ...

Suddenly the junkyard is filled with discarded absinthe bottles. With briar pipes. With fields of writhing and stinking Corpse flowers in full bloom ...

Antique Victrolas and undersized suits ...

Empty bullet shells and musty textbooks ...

There's a rusting *Airstream* over there ...

Flickering fiery shadows on Plato's cave wall ...

"I SAID ... WHATCHYOO DOIN' HERE?" Hitler is furious. His face morphs and blurs, eyes slipping down onto cheeks, nose twisting, mouth widening to infinity ...

Hiram draws his gun and drops it. Loses it among the rubble and debris.

"What the—" Hitler cries, his voice echoing in Hiram's brain. "What're-yoo- What're-yoo ... fucked up-fucked up? You can't-You can't-You can't ...?"

Hiram swings wide. Misses.

"Hey now!" Hitler hollers. "HEY now!"

Hiram lunges. Manages, just barely, to grab the loose strap of Hitler's overalls. Inches his fingers towards Hitler's throat. Intent on choking the life out of him.

But Junkyard Hitler is strong.

He fights back.

Hiram feels punch after punch, blow after blow, landing on his swollen, poisoned, drug-abused belly ... smashing his nose ... boxing his ears and walloping his eyes …

He squeezes, but Hitler won't die. His throat, firm and thick as a log.

Hiram twists, but Hitler's neck won't break.

Hitler grips Hiram by the sides of his head. Strong handfuls of ears and hair. Thumbs reaching towards Hiram's eyes.

For what seems like an eternity, the two are locked in a dual death-grip. Then Hitler manages to struggle out a single word:

"*Why?*"

Hiram brings up his aching, poison-swollen knee. Hard between overalled legs, and Hitler goes limp. Drops his hands.

Hiram shoves.

Shoves the barrel-chested man over the precipice of rusting debris. Sends him sliding down a hill of jagged metal, broken glass and poking wire.

Sends him tumbling to the bears.

In the junkyard office (just a corrugated metal shack on the corner of the twenty ruined acres), Hiram finds a working refrigerator.

Hoping against hope for more whisky. Or another dose of anti-venom. Or water—his throat is parched, raw, burning … He tears out shelves. Tosses aside months-old cartons of Chinese. Sifts through shingles of petrified pizza …

No booze. No anti-venom.

No water.

Nothing even edible—except for one unopened bottle of strange, viscous red liquid: *Clamato*™.

Hiram squints at the label …

> *Clamato is a high-quality, savory tomato*
> *and clam juice cocktail with spices.*

And in the rusty icebox, hidden behind a frost-bitten mountain of unidentifiable veggies: A half-empty bottle of vodka.

Absolut.

As Hiram staggers out of the junkyard, sipping his *Clamato*™ Bloody Mary, he can still hear the bears having their way with Hitler.

Crunching bones, tearing meat and muscle and denim ...

Every now and then Hiram catches sight of a body part, tossed vigorously up into the sky—leaving a trail of splashing blood against the clear blue sky before falling back down, down into the den of the bears ...

On his third grade report card, Hitler's teacher remarked that Adolf was: *'bad tempered and fancied himself a leader.'* True fact.

UberNacht is strangely silent. Mr. Smalls is not at his post by the door.

Inside, Hiram watches the nubile dancers writhing and pressing against each other. They seem strangely subdued. The poison coursing through his system mutes any sense of erotic desire he might otherwise have mustered.

He'd thought for a time that he was dying—despite the initial promise of the anti-venom and whisky. But now he thinks he'll live. He's sick, but he'll live.

He's been sitting at the bar of *UberNacht* for hours—thinking that if he was going to die, he wanted it to be here.

Drinking and waiting … for what, he didn't know.

Drowning his sorrows …

But Sadie is nowhere in sight.

Dark thoughts are creeping in from all sides. Ganging up and surrounding him. Dragging him down into their mean vortex—

> *Mommy's dead and Daddy's gone,*
> *And your baby's gonna be,*
> *The demon's spawn …*

—Hiram sighs. Supposes it's time to head down to the storage room. Force the location of the final little Hitler out of Edsel. And then …

… and then Sadie. Talk with Sadie. Recant his decision. Break his promise to her, keep his promise to Edsel Hitler. Live up to his dark side. Be the monster they expect him to be—

Hiram the devil,
Hiram the Bad …
You really can't mourn the loss of
What you ne'er had …

—his iPhone is chirping. He answers it. Slides heavily off of his barstool, heads for the storage room.

"Hiram? Are you there? It's Mrs. Bothwell."

"Mrs. *Bothwell* … No *Gashleycrumb*?" Hiram teases.

"Listen, Hiram. Don't ask, don't tell. But we've taken care of your '*Jodie Incident.*' Ms. Foster shouldn't be a problem anymore, as long as you … Well, I do hope that there won't be any future … incidents."

"No, ma'am," Hiram is stepping through the back door, heading for the back stairs.

"Anyway, you are free to return home. They—the authorities—won't bother you again, so long as you don't bother her … 'Kay, Sugar?"

"Thank you," Hiram mutters, descending the stairs.

"No prob," Mrs. Bothwell answers. "When you're up for it, we need to speak. Seems there's a growing conflux of SHC activity near Athens—it's the spontaneous human combustion that started the forest fires that are all over the news … So come on down to the office and we'll talk, okay Hon?"

Hiram is about to hang up the phone when she continues speaking.

"Oh! By the way, Hiram," Mrs. Bothwell offhandedly implores. "Who's Gashleycrumb?"

Hiram stops in his tracks. Standing in front of the storage room door, staring at the phone in his hand. His mind is whirling, exhausted from left-over drugs and unanswered questions. Panic is rising.

Who's Gashleycrumb?

Suddenly, a flood of heavy footsteps is rushing down the stairs behind him.

A trap.

Hiram kicks open the supply room door. Lunges inside.

Edsel Hitler is chained to the shelves.

So is Sadie.

Seated in the middle of the room is another Hitler—the last of the twelve.

The final Hitler is wearing nothing but an oversized baby's diaper and a bib. Sitting in an adult-sized baby's high chair. A half-empty baby bottle on the high chair's tray.

Hitler holds a pacifier—a baby's rubber nipple, his *BINKY*—and gestures with it provocatively. As if to say, 'Surprised, old man?'

Behind Hiram, seven bouncers from upstairs—Mr. Smalls among them—storm into the room. Tommy guns held tightly at their sides. Dressed in full Nazi regalia.

"The *UberNacht*," laughs Hitler, spreading his arms to the room. "The perfect place to begin building my army ..."

Beside him, in an enormous crib, are crates stamped *C4 Explosive* and an oversized, plush teddy bear. A gigantic jack-in-the-box frenetically bobs its goofy head. Rattles and crayons, bibs and blocks, litter the floor.

Despite his obvious baby fetish, little Hitler's facial expression betrays a look of cunning and malice. Edsel is staring at him with a look of unrecognizing horror.

Adolf Hitler had strange, decadent desires in the bedroom—he enjoyed being urinated and defecated on. True fact.

Like lightning, Hitler draws a knife from the tray of the high chair and holds it to Sadie's head.

Feeling like he's underwater, in poisoned slow motion, Hiram draws the *Webley*. Takes aim—point blank between Hitler's eyes. Pulls the trigger.

But he knows before the hammer even falls—feels in the nauseous pit of his stomach—that his attempt will fail.

Click.

His mother's shell. The *suicide shell.*

Hitler laughs. A Nazi bouncer steps forward and takes the *Webley* from Hiram. Two more grip him securely by the arms.

"My dear Hiram," Hitler muses. "The true evil at work in the Holocaust wasn't the insanity of Adolf Hitler, but that he could get so many others to follow him …" Hitler sucks on his binky. Smacks it between his lips. Removes it with a *pop!* "Let's see if we can't do it all over again …!"

The two bouncers release Hiram's arms and raise their tommy guns inches from his head. Two more are trained on Sadie.

Hitler burps. A long, loud, raucous belch. Green bubbles float from between his lips and drift languidly about the room, heading up toward the ceiling.

Hiram's hand slides carefully into his pocket. His fingers silently snap open the pillbox.

He takes hold of *The Big H.*

Green bubbles drifting towards him, lazily circling his head.

Hitler burps again. More bubbles.

Hiram rolls the pill nervously between thumb and finger. Cups it in his palm. Slowly removes his hand from his pocket.

A bubble drifts in front of Hiram's eyes. In it, he's astonished to see another eye peering out … bloodshot and circled in green, puckered flesh.

Hiram brings his hand casually to his mouth as if in astonishment. As if to muffle a burp, stifle a yawn.

He pops the pill.

Swallows. The oversized pill sticks in his throat and then dislodges, burning all the way down. The drugs explode in his stomach. Long, fast tendrils reach expertly into his brain, strangling his heart, pressing his lungs. Hiram knows instantly that popping the pill was a mistake.

Another trap.

Hitler laughs. His exposed flesh is turning subtle shades of olive. His voice takes on an unearthly chorus. *"Popped the pill, eh Mr. Grange? The BIG H ...!"* La Fée Verte, speaking through his donkey-punched little green Hitler clone. His chosen one.

His puppet.

"What is it?" Hiram shoves two fingers down his own throat. Trying to gag, knowing it's too late.

The demon laughs.

"It's the Final Solution, Mr. Grange. The trooth, da whole trooth, and nuttin' but da trooth ..."

"Poison?"

Laughing green eyes peering out from a dozen drifting bubbles. *"In a manner of speaking. Poison of the mind. Poison of the soul. The Final Solution. What can be more poison than the Truth?"*

"What's in it?" Hiram is sweating profusely, beginning to tremble.

"DMT, among other things. The strongest psychedelic known to man, fire-brewed in the human pineal gland at the forty-ninth day after conception. Mixed with a generous dose of Sodium Pentothal—God's own truth serum ...

"A religious experience in capsule form, don'tcha know? Integrated with a transcendental trip compliments of the G-Men at Operation Mindfuck. *And all wrapped up nicely in an irresistible compulsion to tell—and more importantly, to see—only the truth! The trooth, da whole trooth, and nuttin' but da trooth...!*

"Ready to talk, Mr Grange? Ready to get real?"

Hiram says nothing. The drugs are taking hold fast. Tearing his mind apart, shredding his ego. There's no fighting them. No fighting the truth—the truth that is slowly filling his head, pushing everything else out.

"We all live in the shadow of the things we've done," the demon

implores. "*Look at the monuments and pebbles of your own past ... And tell me, Hiram. Tell me: How dark is your heart? Hiram? How dim is your soul?*"

Hiram opens his mouth to speak, but the demon shushes him with a wave of Hitler's hand. "*Don't answer. It was rhetorical. Now, what say we get down to brass tacks?*

"*You've murdered ten innocents. Haven't you?*"

"Yes," says Hiram.

"*Ten innocent little Hitlers,*" Hitler grins, exposing a wide smile of green demon-teeth. Belches another burst of tiny green bubbles. "*And you want to kill to more. Don't you? You want to kill more ...*"

"Yes," answers Hiram.

"*And for what?*" La Fée Verte laughs maniacally. "*Because an anonymous e-mail told you to? An e-mail from Yours Truly? La Fée Gashleycrumb ... Is that really it? Is that why you kill, Hiram?*"

"No."

"*Then why, Hiram? Why?*"

A tear escapes the corner of Hiram's eye. Slides down his cheek. "It's my nature," he whispers. "I'm a killer ..."

The demon giggles. "*What now, Hiram? No time for bullshit. What does your black heart tell you? Hmm? You can't lie to me. The Sodium Pentothal won't let you ... You can't lie to yourself ... Tell me, Hiram. Tell us all. What do you want?*"

Hiram slumps to the floor. "I want to die without knowing I ever lived ..." he says. "Everything I am, everything I've done ... I don't want to take it with me ... I want to leave it behind ... I want to disappear." He looks at Sadie, at her belly. Cradles his head in his hands. "All I want is to disappear ... disappear and to never have existed at all." He is weeping openly now.

Hitler has turned a darker shade of green. Lets loose another loud, bubbling belch.

La Fée Verte continues to watch—smiling, gleeful eyes peering out from countless green bubbles.

"*If that's what you want,*" the demon speaks through Hitler. "*If that's what you really, really want ...*" Hitler hands Hiram his gun.

The *Webley* feels solid, heavy in his hand.

Hiram raises the gun to his head.

Cocks the hammer.

"*Oh my, oh my!*" cries the demon. "*Wait just a second! We forgot one thing!*"

One of the uniformed bouncers uncuffs Sadie. She collapses into Hiram's arms.

The drugs are dissolving his brain. Hiram is losing himself to the truth—untamed and out of control Truth ...

"How can you disappear without ever having existed—without leaving a trace—when ..." *La Fée Verte* licks his green Hitler-lips and turns his beady eyes downward. Lands his gaze directly on Sadie, on her still-flat baby belly.

There's no more will, no more control. Hiram is a slave to his animal needs. His genetic flotsam. His guttural, unspoken fears. A slave to the truth.

"*You hold two mirrors perfectly facing one another ...*" the demon muses. "*What's on them?*"

"*We die to remember what we live to forget ...*"

Sadie tilts her head, her eyes meet Hiram's. Her nose is running, her voice is trembling. "Her name, Hiram ... Her name ... Or *his* name ..." Her eyes are watery. A lone tear rolls down her cheek and over Hiram's fingers. "His name is going to be Atlhea ..." She folds her fingers over Hiram's. "*Atlhea* ... Short for *And They Lived Happily Ever After ...*"

Hiram raises the gun to Sadie's head.

Places his other hand on her never-to-be-swollen belly.

There is no choice. There is only the rush of Sodium Pentothal truth. The dissolving of ego. The dissolution of time. The abandonment of morality.

"My life is nothing but monsters, Sadie ..." Hiram is weeping now. "Monsters and violence ... I have more nightmares than I do memories ..."

There is only the truth.

The Big H ...

The Final Solution ...

Hiram slides the barrel up to Sadie's temple ...

... and pulls the trigger.

He pulls the trigger and—*BLAM!*—he condemns himself to hell.

Everything is different now.

How could he let this happen ... how could he *make* this happen?

How could he *want* this?

How could he live with himself?

Hiram raises the gun to his own temple. Tears stream down his cheeks. 'I'm sorry, Sadie ... I'm so sorry ...' he cries.

Pulls the trigger.

Click.

The empty shell? No, he'd already fired his mother's shell at Hitler, when he'd first stormed into the room ...

He pulls the trigger again.

Click.

And again. *Click.*

"Fuck!" he screams. Throws the gun away.

Sadie is dead in his lap. Her blood on his shirt. His unborn son ...

Dead. All dead.

The demon is laughing. In his outstretched palm he holds the four unfired shells. "*And the corruption of Hiram Grange is complete ...!*"

La Fée Verte cackles. The Potential Future is no more—*Hiram the White, Hiram the Holy* ... both fade into the foggy quantum nothingness of *Hiram the Never-Will-Be* ...

Hiram looks up through his burning tears to see Edsel slowly reaching, reaching for the tommy gun at the belt of the bouncer nearest him. Fingers slowly groping, he quickly grasps the weapon and yanks it free.

Guns down the surprised bouncer.

Sprays bullets into the kneecaps of the startled rest—Mr. Smalls falls to the floor, writhing in blood, bone fragments and pain. His eyes are wide with shock and surprise. "WHAT?" he cries. "WHERE AM I?"

Edsel turns the gun on the green, bubble-spewing Hitler. Shoots his evil, demon-possessed brother. Point blank, in the head. Empties the clip.

Hitler's cranium explodes.

As he dies, the demon-bubbles burst, showering the room in green liquid flame.

Instantly, the supply room is engulfed in fire. The Nazi bouncers, broken from their spell, desperately crawl for the door. Shattered knees leaving thick trails of blood on the floor. Green napalm burning their backs.

Hiram cradles his dear, dead Sadie in his arms. Tries to kiss her back to life. Through the smoke and flames he hears a terrified mewling. He calls to Boo the kitty, but the cat has already fled.

"Help me," calls Edsel weakly. Chained to the smoldering shelves. "I don't want to die ..."

Resting Sadie's head gently on the floor of her *UberNacht*, Hiram rises to his feet.

Digs the keys from his pocket and uncuffs Edsel.

For a moment, they lock eyes. Green fire rages all around them.

"Go," Hiram tells him. "Go far away. Lose yourself. Maybe Anchorage, maybe Mexico … I never want to see you again." He shoves the last little Hitler towards the door. Fire is creeping along the ceiling.

"Oh," Hiram calls out to him through the flame and smoke. "One more thing … You might want to think about changing your name …"

Hitler smiles, turns, and is gone.

Hiram sits down to die. Waiting for the flames to take him—incinerate him, as if he'd never existed.

But through the smoke comes a voice. A voice, and that unmistakable feeling of being watched.

"Get up, Hiram." The voice is gravely, but vaguely feminine. "Get a hold of yourself. I'm here to help."

"Leave me," Hiram sits firm.

"I can't. You're needed elsewhere, but that's all I can tell you …"

"Are you my deus ex machina?" The Sodium Pentothal is wearing off. The drugs, the psychedelic fingerprint, are taking hold again. But weaker than before. The smoke is choking his lungs. "Are you my guardian angel?"

"Nothing is as it seems," the gravely voice tells him. "The Cascade has advanced, and time is growing short. Your job is far from over."

The shadowy figure reaches towards Hiram. He reaches back, but instead of taking his hand she places the *Webley* firmly into it. Through the smoke and tears and inferno, Hiram can only make out a vague silhouette. He climbs to his feet on wobbly legs.

"Come on. This bar's coming down all around us …"

Hiram's savior turns to the door. Tendrils of flame are creeping up its frame. Creeping across the floor. Licking Sadie's blood-mottled hair, her skirt, her flesh.

"Follow me," the stranger insists. Hiram tears his eyes away from his dead almost-lover. Does as he's told, follows the stranger. She leads him through smoke and fire. Past crumbling walls, collapsing ceilings.

She leads him to safety.

Outside, Hiram heaves cool air into his choked, burning lungs.

"I wanted to die in there …" he says, but she is gone.

With an infernal blast, the C4 in the supply room detonates and the *UberNacht* crumbles to the ground. Burying Sadie—burying his unborn son—in embers and flame.

Hiram is desperately tired. And empty. And heartbroken.

And hungry.

Tomorrow he will see Mrs. Bothwell. Tomorrow there will be another mission …

But for now …

For now *The Binge* is finally behind him.

The long fall and loop-de-loop are over. He'd lost so much—lost everything—and pulled out just before hitting rock bottom. Like he always does …

For now, he plans to find an all-night diner and eat until his stomach is full. Eat until he can eat no more. Gyros and gravy fries, egg creams and sodas, burgers and buffalo wings and tacos … Filling his stomach where he cannot fill his soul.

Sadie had said that only he had the power to forgive himself. Maybe someday he would …

Epilogue

In our world, Boo the kitty bears sole witness to the subtle rip in Reality, and the green eye peeking out. Sitting a safe distance from the smoldering remains of *UberNacht*, the cat watches the watching eye until the slit in Reality suddenly shifts—slides quickly away through the night and is gone.

In our world, the cat sits on its haunches and stares for a long while at the place where the rip had been. Then turns to the place where *UberNacht* lies in smoking ruins—where a new Confluence had very nearly opened up. Then the feline twitches its whiskers, licks its chops and struts off.

Boo'd had his fill of this craziness. He'd put off his cat business long enough. It was time to be getting back home—back home to West Searsville Road.

In the Abyss, *La Fée Verte* grins as Hiram places a bouquet of Corpse flowers on Sadie's unmarked grave. The demon's pupil dilates behind its latest cosmetic addition: a single-spectacled, thick-rimmed eyeglass, fuzzy black caterpillar eyebrow and waxy false Groucho Marx mustache.

'*Untils we meets again, silly man,*' the demon cackles. Emits a raucous Bronx Cheer.

'*Pbtbtbtbtbbtbt …!*'

"*Wheeeeeee …!*"

Then *La Fée Verte* turns its gaze westward, dragging the tear in the epidermis of Reality with it. Ever westward …

All the way to Graceland.

Memphis, Tennessee ... where, even now, twelve white-suited, bell-bottomed, knee-bobbing, hip-thrusting, lip-curling, porkchop-sideburned embryos in diamond-studded diapers, white silk jumpsuits, are sleeping innocently in twelve bubbling, glass vats ...

AUTHOR'S NOTE

*The bulk of this novel was written over the course of a 14-day water fast.
The author apologizes for any unnecessary dalliance
on the subjects of diet and cuisine.*

SCOTT CHRISTIAN CARR

Scott Christian Carr's fiction has appeared in dozens of magazines and publications, including *Shroud Magazine*, *GUD*, *Pulp Eternity*, *Horror Quarterly*, *The Dream People Literary Magazine*, *The MUFON Journal* and *Withersin*. His novella *A Helmet Full of Hair* was recently translated and reprinted in the prestigious French quarterly, *Galaxies La Revue de Référence de la Science Fiction*.

In 1999 Scott was awarded The Hunter S. Thompson Award for Outstanding Journalism, in 2006 his original television pilot *The REAL Deal* was awarded 1st Place in *Scriptapalooza TV* for Best Original Pilot, in 2009 he was a contributor to the Bram Stoker Award-nominated *Beneath the Surface* (Shroud Publishing), and he is a 2010 *Choate Road* "Spotlight Scribe."

He is currently pushing his latest novel *The First Time We Died* out into the world, and diving into his next: *The Apocalypse Will Be Televised: A Reality Television Tragedy*.

Scott lives on a secluded mountaintop in New York's Hudson Valley with his wife Amy and two children, Emmett and Eden. He writes every day.

Visit him on-line at *www.scottchristiancarr.com*.

BOOK 1

Jake Burrows

Hiram Grange & the Village of the Damned

Something wicked walks the streets of the picturesque New
Hampshire village of Great Bay—something that has inexplicably
risen from the grave to wreak a horrifying vengeance.
Only one man can stop it—Hiram Grange—provided he can sober
up long enough to answer the call!

BOOK 2

Scott Christian Carr

Hiram Grange & the Twelve Little Hitlers

Hitler has escaped. Twelve of them, to be precise, each cloned from
the original, and hiding in the bizarre American underground.
Hiram Grange has been tasked with hunting them down.
The only problem: he's hit rock bottom. His worst binge ever—
a mad dance with absinthe, opium and depression …

BOOK 3

Robert Davies

Hiram Grange & the Digital Eucharist

From its global headquarters in Boston, the mysterious
Occlusionist Movement is preparing to control the world with
its Digital Eucharist, while in the serpentine bowels of the city an
ancient demon is unleashed, eager for revenge against the man who
imprisoned it years ago—Hiram Grange!

HIRAM GRANGE

BOOK 4

Kevin Lucia

Hiram Grange & the Chosen One

Hiram Grange doesn't believe in fate. He makes his own destiny.
That's a good thing, because Queen Mab of Faerie has foreseen the
destruction of the world, and as usual ... it's all Hiram's fault.
He must choose: kill an innocent girl and save the universe ...
or rescue her and watch all else burn.
Just another day on the job for Hiram Grange.

BOOK 5

Richard Wright

Hiram Grange & the Nymphs of Krakow

Hiram Grange was already broken when his world was turned
upside down by the horrifying revelations of a beautiful and
dangerous woman. Faced with the possibility that he's been a pawn
in a diabolical game, he seeks the truth in the snows of Krakow.
But the truth is guarded by ancient, winged things,
and the truth has teeth ...

WWW.HIRAMGRANGE.COM

Also from Shroud Publishing ...

Maurice Broaddus • *Devil's Marionette*

Death comes for the cast and crew of the hit comedy TV Show Chocolate City, impacting not only their personal lives but the prospect of their show's continued success. As each member sinks into their own past, and the spirits of those that came before, the tragedies continue.

When your terror comes to claim you, who will it be? *Nobody.*

R. Scott McCoy • *FEAST*

Deputy Sheriff Nick Ambrose can look into someone's eyes and glimpse their guilt, to an extent. But when he and his brother take on a psychopathic killer, he gains something more: the ability to see, and devour, souls. Plagued by this terrifying new power, and by the spirits of both his brother and the butcher trapped inside his mind, he sets out to understand and control his new fate and to grapple with the shadowy auras he now sees all around.

Can he command the darkness welling within, or will he become merely its vessel?

Cindy Little • *Intruder*

When the powers of an ancient malevolent creature invade a quiet suburban household, a young mother is forced into a pitched battle for the life of her child.

Rio Youers • *Mama Fish*

At Harlequin High School In 1986, Kelvin Fish is the oddball, the weird kid that no one will talk to, except for Patrick Beauchamp, who is determined to learn more. When Patrick's curiosity leads him into a bizarre and tragic series of events, he gets much more than he bargained for.

D. Harlan Wilson • *Peckinpah: An Ultraviolent Romance*

Life in Dreamfield is a daily harangue of pigs, cornfields, pigs, fast food joints, pigs, Dollar Stores, pigs, motorcycles, pigs, and good old-fashioned Amerikan redneckery. Angry, slick-talking, and ultraviolent to the core, Samson Thataway and the Fuming Garcias commit art-for-art's-sake in the form of hideous, unmotivated serial killings. When an unsuspecting everyman's wife is murdered by the throng, it is up to Felix Soandso to avenge her death and return Dreamfield to its natural state of absurdity.

SHROUD Magazine

Published quarterly, SHROUD contains the latest pulse-pounding stories from the masters of the genre. Fiction, art, book reviews, films, and insightful articles that pull back the veil separating fantasy from reality. Shocking, cerebral and satisfying.

Available now at www.shroudmagazine.com

Made in the USA
Charleston, SC
04 January 2010